A DANGEROUS ELEMENT

Gregory S. Lamb

Happy Reading

20 FEB 2014

Cover Design by Kit Foster

DEDICATION

To Matisse, man's best friend.

ACKNOWLEDGMENTS

My wife Cynthia is and has always been an inspiration. She dedicated much of her spare time to reading and editing some of my early work and provided me with the safe, quiet space and time needed to write A Dangerous Element. Without the attention of Raymond Vogel, Oliver "Frank" Chase, and Ryan Attard, along with the rest of the team from AEC Stellar Inc, I don't think this book would have made it to press. I appreciate the time, patience, and advice they so unselfishly provided.

A big shout out to my Beta Readers, Paul Memrick and James Crocker. Laura Smith and Nicole Higgins from the Orchard Book Club for offering your unbiased feedback and some initial edits that I didn't expect or ask for but really needed and appreciated. If you like the cover, credit goes to Kit Foster from Kit Foster Cover Designs. Kit is one of the easiest to work with artists I could have hoped for.

Enjoy the story.

*TOP SECRET/SCI: MV-ULTRA *

DTG 041955z1211

Classification// TS/SCI: MV-ULTRA/ Eyes Only

//FM: ██████/field Ops/CIA//

//TO: ██████████/Deputy Director/OGA/Mid-East Field Desk//

//SUBJ: TARGET STATUS REPORT//

A. BETHESDA NAVAL HOSPITAL (WARD 8)

1. Target -███████████ arrived 48HRs ago in good health. No physical wounds observed from extraction operations. ████████ appears to have no recollection of ████████████ ████████████████. He is guarded and unresponsive to questions and required group session activities.

2. Primary target control subject, Lance Corporal ██████████ arrived approximately one day prior to ████████. ██████ psychotic behavioral and hallucination symptoms responded well to medication. █████ has no recollection of events prior to being detained.

3. Blood and urine samples taken with lab results consistent with MV-ULTRA residuals.

4. 24HR Surveillance Team is in place and will continue to act as courier for further reporting.

//END OF MSG//

*TOP SECRET/SCI: MV-ULTRA *

Handle VIA EYES ONLY - DESTROY IMMEDIATLY AFTER READING

Chapter 1

4 December 2011 - Bethesda Naval Hospital

The combination of rattling window blinds and the bright light that broke through them was too much. Mark struggled for a moment with sleep and then cracked open his mouth to breath. The air tasted sterile, like lemons and rubbing alcohol. He rolled away from the light and peered through heavy eyelids at the shadow nearby. It was a slender young man wearing a dark blue uniform – a Navy uniform. The metal corpsman badge glinted in stark contrast.

"Who are you?" He asked. "And where is this place?"

"Sir, please get up and come with me. We need to take another blood sample," the Navy corpsman said.

Mark swiveled himself to the edge of the bed and slipped his bare feet into a pair of disposable slippers. He stood, rubbing his tired eyes with his left hand, and then noticed a sudden throbbing ache behind his left ear. He reached around to see what was causing it, and the pain of touching it made him wince.

"Are you going to answer me?" Mark was used to getting answers. Being a Colonel in the United States Air Force came with answers. He eyed the young man and waited.

"Sir, you're at Bethesda Naval Hospital. Ward 8. Don't you remember our conversation last night? You were cracking me up."

"No, I don't remember anything like that. How'd I get here, anyway?"

"We'll get to that. First, let's take care of the blood sample. The lab is just across the hall. It will only take a minute or two. I guess you don't remember we did this drill last night, aye?"

Mark didn't say anything. He got up and followed the corpsman, who was holding the door open while pointing in the direction of the lab. With a glance down the corridor, Mark saw half a dozen security guards, fit and alert, standing together near an external door. They looked to be mostly Marine and Army. In the other direction was a much different line – one full of white pajamas and blue hospital robes that matched his own. Their line led to a window labeled "Pharmacy" in faded, black letters.

"A psych ward," Mark said under his breath.

"Sir?" asked the corpsman.

Mark didn't reply. They stepped into the adjacent lab, and he sat in the nearest chair.

"Sir, it isn't anything to be embarrassed about. Really. You

3

wouldn't believe who I've seen come through here."

"What do you mean?"

"Well, a guy like you in a mental hospital. It's just a precaution, I can assure you."

Mark was familiar with psych wards. Years back, he'd had the opportunity to observe a similar ward in the hospital at Walter Reed. Places like this were like a jail. A jail with treatment that wasn't optional.

The lab technician finally seemed to notice them. He slid his wheeled chair over and began to prep Mark's arm with practiced efficiency.

"Last night you were hallucinating, saying all kinds of weird things. You don't remember any of it?"

Mark looked back at the corpsman and shook his head. It was an answer, of sorts, but mostly he was trying to clear his mind. Everything was still too close to being a dream.

"Does the name Snake mean anything to you?"

Only his years of experience in the field kept Mark from knocking the technician onto his back and throwing an elbow into the chin of the corpsman. Just hearing the name Snake made his instincts cry out for action. Instead, he made a casual scan of his surroundings and focused on slowing his heart rate.

"Anyway, we can talk more later. Looks like we're done here. Thanks, Frank."

The technician nodded, and Mark felt himself being helped back to his feet.

"You can line up with the others for meds," the corpsman said.

"What?"

"Your medicine. Just jump in line there with the others. To your left when you step into the hall. "

Mark followed Frank's instructions and lined up with the others. He knew there was no choice in the matter, despite the friendly tone. But he also knew there was no way he was taking any meds until he found out more about where he was – and why he was there.

The next morning, Mark settled into what would become a daily routine. It was a group therapy session, a ragtag crew of men and women who met in the common room to take turns explaining why they thought they had been hospitalized. Mark picked up his workbook and took a seat. He noticed that some of the patients were wearing their military uniforms, only with slippers instead of their boots. He was still in hospital garb, as were a few others that looked like recent arrivals.

"Okay, I'm Marine Lance Corporal, Ronny Clark." The young man's voice betrayed his anger and frustration, despite his efforts to appear calm. "I've been here for fifteen days, now. I was hearing voices and things on the radio. Stories in the news kept telling me to watch out because there are people who want to kill me."

The other patients sitting among the circle of misfits weren't paying attention. Mark feigned his own disinterest, but he was listening carefully to every word.

"These people you were hearing, did they address you by your name?" asked the group therapist.

"I just said that, didn't I? I said that yesterday and the day before, too," Ronny replied.

"Did you recognize any of the voices?"

"The voices sounded familiar, but I don't know from where. Anyway, when am I getting out of here?"

The therapist didn't answer and instead, quickly turned to the next patient.

Mark didn't believe in coincidence. He had a pretty good idea what would happen if he gave any indication he experienced symptoms similar to Ronny's. While the others were listening to the next patient, Mark let his mind wander back to better days.

Mark let himself believe that he and his family enjoyed happier times before his being assigned to Langley Air Force Base as a Headquarters Staff Officer. The job was nothing special, just a holding pattern for him until he could return to the cockpit of his A-10 "Warthog." Ultimately, he wanted to command a squadron, and that was something he couldn't do from behind a desk.

His memories from the days when he was still flying his A-10 were good. He was still married and a father to Jenna and Suzy. His work days ended in hugs and kisses, and his weekends were filled with playground trips and birthday parties.

Being assigned to a staff job was just the beginning - it was the brainstorming session with Snake that had changed everything. That was where he had first learned of the new form of weapon they were working on.

His thoughts were broken by a change in speaker, and he was once again sitting in his plastic chair and staring down at his workbook. The session dragged on through two more patients until they were finally released.

Mark spent the remainder of the day pondering his predicament, trying to piece together how he had gotten there, and what to do about it. He wasn't exactly sure how he'd been targeted, but he was familiar with the methods for using the weapon. It was used with a "control," and Mark was pretty sure the weapon was also used on Ronny Clark.

Finally, while staring at the blank, white wall of his hospital room that evening, Mark realized his only option was to escape and that Ronny was going to help him.

***

"Game of Chess?" Mark asked.

Ronny pushed his chair back and stood up behind the empty table, "No, sir, not today. Not if you're just going to let me win again. That'd be three days in a row."

"You think that's what's been happening here?" Mark asked as he sat across from the young Marine, gesturing for him to be seated. "No way I'd let you win. You're talented. What are you, twenty years old or something?"

"Nineteen, sir," Ronny replied.

Mark set the board and pieces on the table. Before they had everything set up, they were interrupted by a woman's voice trying to get everyone's attention. Mark looked up and saw a female orderly standing near the entryway, with one of her hands resting on the doorjamb.

"Anyone need a smoke break?" she asked in soft voice, unable to get everyone's attention.

An older Navy Petty Officer, overweight with wispy, grey sideburns, grunted as he got his feet. Then, he sauntered over toward the orderly.

"You did say 'smoke break,' am I correct?" he asked.

Ronny looked anxious. "Sir, can we do this in a little while? I think I'm going to join them," he said. He sounded a little embarrassed.

Mark spotted the telltale shape of a cigarette pack in Ronny's shirt pocket. "I think I'd like to come along. Mind if I bum one from you? I'll make it up, I promise."

"Sure, sir. No problem. I never met a Colonel who smoked. Didn't think it was politically correct," Ronny said.

Before being escorted out of the building, the orderly took the four of them to another room where she unlocked the door and switched on the overhead fluorescents. On the shelves inside, there were clear, plastic bins with nametags for each of the patients. Mark could see shaving supplies, bootlaces, and even rank insignia inside them. Ronny took down a clipboard to sign out a BIC lighter. The process seemed like a big production, but he wasn't going to miss an opportunity to take a look at the outside of the building.

Walking through the corridor of the hospital lobby on the main floor, Mark felt the curious stares of the regular patients and visitors in waiting areas.

The orderly held the door open for them. Mark shrugged as he walked past her through the door. The air was brisk, but not enough to disguise the smell of stale cigarette ash and the accumulated filth of vehicle exhaust. He noted the smoking area placard on the side of the concrete parking garage. It reminded him that to discourage smoking, military commanders made it a point of establishing designated smoking areas in the least attractive locations possible.

Mark made a quick survey of his surroundings. There were

cameras at each corner of the garage, but he couldn't spot any other security or surveillance.

Ronny pulled the pack from his shirt pocket and shook a couple of cigarettes out of the corner. He took one for himself, then passed the pack over to Mark.

"Thanks," Mark said, taking the offering.

Ronny lit up then handed his lighter to Mark.

"I get out tomorrow. They haven't told me what time, though," Ronny said.

"I figured. Couldn't see any reason for them to keep you. There isn't anything wrong with you," Mark said. Whatever might actually be wrong with Ronny, Mark knew it was the same thing wrong with himself. He only hoped it wasn't anything more serious.

"I still can't explain the weird delusions, though," Ronny said. He sounded troubled about it. "They seemed so real at the time. It was pretty scary. I wish they'd let me back in my unit. I'll get transferred as soon as I get there, though. Marines don't like having damaged goods in their mix. It wouldn't be an issue if I got shot up or something, but Marines can't deal with psych stuff. It freaks 'em out."

"It doesn't matter what branch of the service you're in, the military doesn't like defects," Mark said. He kept his tone matter-of-fact. Ronny needed his help, he just didn't know it yet. "But you're not defective, kid. You can re-invent yourself in your new unit after you're transferred. Who knows, things might go better for you."

Ronny cracked a smile and exhaled a fountain of white smoke through his teeth. It lingered in the cold air, so he blew it away before speaking. "Thanks, sir. You know how it is, not knowing what is going to happen next. Ever since boot camp, I've gotten used to having a pretty tight plan."

Before finishing their smokes, Mark turned to Ronny. "There's a convenience store run this afternoon. I'll replace the cigarettes before you go."

"That'd be nice, sir, but you don't have to."

"I want to. Besides, we'll be taking another break after dinner."

"Sir, they won't let you go to the store if you don't fill out your workbook during group. It's one of their unspoken rules. They'll also let you wear your uniform again. It took me ten days before I figured that one out. They don't tell you either."

Mark clapped Ronny on the shoulder, "Thanks. That's good to know."

Just when the orderly announced that it was time to go inside, Mark noticed a vehicle departing from the lower deck of the adjacent parking garage. It looked out of place. There were two close-cropped occupants in the front seats. Both wore identical suits and wrap-around sunglasses.

"Never trust anyone who drives a black Escalade and wears sunglasses on a gloomy day," Mark said.

Ronny moved beside Mark to watch. As he did, the Escalade accelerated out of the parking garage and onto the main road with a screech.

"What was that all about?" Ronny asked.

"Just the wheels of Washington D.C., always around to remind us we're not really in charge of anything," Mark replied. He watched until the SUV had fully disappeared from view.

When it came time for the afternoon group session, Mark obediently filled out the questionnaire in his workbook. He even made his best effort to sound genuine when it was his turn to speak.

"I'm here because I was hallucinating. I had strange visions and even started hearing things. I think the meds are working. I'm finally starting to feel like my old self again. It's been quite a relief, actually."

The facilitator showed signs of approval, then moved on to the next patient.

After the session, Mark watched the care team doctors and analysts go into the conference room across from the pharmacy window. He followed the instructions from one of the doctors, to line up in the corridor near the door, along with the other patients.

Mark turned to the patient standing immediately in front of

him and whispered, "This reminds me of elementary school, only I was door monitor, so I always got to be at the front of the line."

"Yeah, well, for me it's just more 'hurry the fuck up and wait,' like I've been doing ever since I enlisted. I fuckin' hate the Army," he said, without even a glance toward Mark.

One of the doctors opened the door, inviting the young Army soldier to enter and leaving Mark at the head of the line.

He waited until the Army soldier left the room before entering. Sitting around the table, Mark saw a mixed team of medical professionals. All of them were wearing the military uniform of their service with their rank prominently worn on their shirt collar or shoulder. He noticed the specialty badges they were all wearing, but was only familiar with the psychologist's badge worn by an African American Captain.

Several of the other medical officers were leafing through manila files containing lab reports. Mark saw the empty chair at the head of the table. An older-looking Navy Commander looked up from his notes and said, "Please, take a seat Colonel. How are things going for you today?"

Mark took his seat as instructed. "Meds must be working. I'm feeling more like my usual self." It was a blatant lie, but he'd spent the back end of his career lying, so it came out naturally and without so much as a nervous blink. He hadn't swallowed a single pill since he'd been given them. He just kept going to the men's room with a cheek full, and nobody seemed to notice.

"Do you feel safe here?" The question came from the psychologist Captain he spotted when he came in.

"Sure."

"What do you think was the cause of your hallucinations, Colonel Reynolds?" asked the Navy Commander sitting to his right.

"I don't know. Maybe something triggered a short circuit in my brain. To be honest, I don't remember anything that happened during the two weeks before I woke up in this place. I was working pretty hard, though. Not much sleep. I guess sleep deprivation can have an effect on the way our brains work." He could see the hidden smirks behind their masks of professionalism. He was saying exactly what they wanted to hear. He wished he had a deck of cards − a few games of poker with these guys would be a nice bonus for his troubles.

"Colonel, you can be excused," the Navy Commander and leader of the care team said. "Please, shut the door on your way out."

A DANGEROUS ELEMENT

//FM: H. Smith/field Ops/CIA//
//TO: R. Wormwood/Deputy Director OGA/Mid-East Field
Desk//Director SpecWar/DARPA
//SUBJ: TARGET STATUS UPDATE//
A. BETHESDA NAVAL HOSPITAL (WARD 8)
1. Target - Colonel Reynolds assessed by psych eval team with no
suspicion of foul play. Reynolds exhibits no recall of events.
Subject is stable but guarded, likely due to prior experience and
training in intelligence operations. Latest blood work indicates no
residuals. MRI assessed as inconclusive.
2. Control subject - Lance Corporal Clark - Safe for release and
discharge from Marine Corps. Will continue to monitor.

//END OF MSG//

"Good evening, this is Brian Williams reporting to you this evening with more developments on Iran..."

Mark entered the dayroom and saw the TV was tuned into NBC's Nightly News. He and the other patients immediately, as if by instinct, focused their attention on the TV when they heard the word "Iran" blaring from the set. Mark set his tray on the nearest table and riveted his eyes and ears to the story.

"The Iranian government is claiming to have shot down an American stealth unmanned combat air vehicle. The clip you're seeing is footage of an American drone taking off from it's base in Kandahar, Afghanistan."

The ticker beneath the clip noted that the aircraft was an "RQ-170 Drone." For Mark, this confirmed a few of the things he'd been piecing together about his situation.

"These next clips aired on Al Jazeera International, shortly after the aircraft was brought down. The Iranian officials broadcasting from the crash sight are seen here brandishing pieces of the aircraft and celebrating. The parts have clear American military markings. If it becomes confirmed that this is our drone and they have intentionally destroyed it, this could represent a violation of national sovereignty and an act of war."

Since the background audio was mostly in Farsi, Mark couldn't confirm the veracity of the story. Instead, he watched the subtitles for anything else that might help him understand what was happening.

"Sir, do you think that UAV was ours?"

Mark recognized Ronny from his voice. "They're called drones now," he answered. "The term 'Unmanned Aerial Vehicles' was dropped from the lexicon after nine-eleven, and no, I don't think there are enough facts to be sure of anything yet. It smacks of politics if you ask me."

Ronny sat beside him, and the two men made quick work of their hospital dinners while the newscasters continued to speculate. As he finished his last bite, however, Mark was distracted by another set of images on the TV.

"Obliques," he said under his breath. He recognized the textures in the images. "Those could only have been grabbed by a U-2 operating off the coast in the Persian Gulf."

"Sir, did you say something?" Ronny asked.

"Shhh. No, just watch."

The images depicted a factory complex that had been destroyed.

"...as you can see in this satellite imagery, our sources have confirmed the centrifuges at a nuclear enrichment facility in Natanz, Iran have mysteriously imploded...."

"Sir , it seems like suddenly there is a lot of bad stuff going down in Iran. Why all of a sudden?" Ronny asked.

Mark knew that Ronny, along with the general population, wouldn't have had a clue about the Top Secret plans for destroying the facility. Instead of opening up a can of worms, he said, "Ever since the hostage crisis in '79, our country has been at odds with Iran. This is nothing new," Mark explained, brushing off any suspicion of interest on his part. "Did you ever find out what time you're leaving tomorrow?"

"Yes, sir," Ronny said. "Right after the care team interview. I haven't been told if I'll be going back as a Marine or a civilian. This whole thing is so messed up." He leaned onto his hands and stared down at his empty food tray.

"Ronny, I like you. I think we can maybe work together to get you heading in the right direction. See these eagles on my shoulders?" Mark pointed to his rank, not expecting Ronny to answer. "I may be a crazy mother fucker stuck in a psych ward, but I still know people, people with influence. Problem is, I can't get to them from here. I could try to make a call or two, but they'll monitor me for sure, and it would only make things worse."

"What do you mean?"

"When you're released tomorrow, we work together. I'm going to take a little hiatus from this place to make a few calls for you. During a smoke break, that way nobody will miss me. You game?"

Ronny nodded. "Just tell me what you want me to do, sir. I've got your back."

Chapter 2

7 December 2011 - Bethesda Naval Hospital

Mark set the paperback he'd been reading down on the bedside table. Out of sheer boredom and the need for a distraction, he had pulled it from the shelf in the dayroom. It was a Clive Cussler novel. The copy was worn, it's pages crumpled and folded from years of handling. He reached over and switched off the bedside lamp.

In the quiet of his room, Mark felt more acutely, the sore spot behind his left ear. It gave him an itching and burning sensation. He put his fingers up to the wound and felt for the scar, then he rolled onto his side to turn the lamp back on. Before getting up, Mark reminded himself of the strong likelihood that he was being watched at all times.

He went into the bathroom to relieve himself before stepping over to the sink to look in the mirror. He saw his own reflection for the first time in weeks. His blue eyes, now bloodshot from the lack of sleep he'd been getting, stared back at him. He noticed the scruffy stubble growing from his unshaven face. There was no sign of grey in the beard that matched his short cropped, light brown hair. Turning his head to the side, he could see that the wound behind his ear wasn't from an accident or any kind of physical encounter. It was a surgical incision and he knew what it meant. He was being tracked.

He switched off the bathroom light and bedside lamp, returning his room to darkness. To avoid any suspicion, he laid on his back for a long while and pretended to doze. When he couldn't keep the ruse going any longer without actually falling asleep, he turned onto his side and pulled the sheet and blanket over his head. He wanted to investigate the incision.

He touched the wound with his fingers. It was tightly stitched and had a pill-shaped lump just beneath the skin. The site of the tracking device was painful to the touch, but he would have kept his touches light regardless. He had to be careful not to cause any bleeding that would raise suspicion. The implant felt like an encased chip. It was larger than the kind he'd seen the veterinarian place into the neck of his family's German Shepherd, now in the custody of his ex-wife and daughters.

Until recently, Mark hadn't thought of Anne or his daughters in a long time. It was probably why his marriage fell apart. There never was any difference between work and off-duty time. Since his early days in Undergraduate Pilot Training, he had been on duty twenty-four seven. He still found time to relax and have a beer with the squadron at the end of a tough week of flying. But to Mark, the social time spent with his peers was part of the job.

He hoped Anne and Charles, her new husband, were safe. He wanted his family to be far enough removed so that they wouldn't be associated with him or put in any danger. If Charles hadn't have relocated the family to Maryland, Mark might not have been as concerned. He guessed that Jenna was ten already, making Suzy almost eight. He'd long since accepted that Charles was a better father for the girls than he'd ever been. Charles treated Anne well, and she seemed happy. It was good for everyone, and it made it all the more easy for Mark to move on.

The new scar behind his ear was a clear indication that he needed to stay far away from them.

***

Ward 8 was still quiet when he awoke. Mark looked through the window and saw a light snow falling. Sitting on the edge of the bed, he reached behind his left ear and gave his head a gentle rub. He had a few things to take care of this morning, if his plan was going to succeed.

Mark went through the meds line and put on his show in

group therapy. Afterward, he retrieved a breakfast tray at another window down the hall before carrying it into the dayroom. When he entered, Mark saw that the other patients were already seated and watching the morning news. Mark sat at a table by himself.

He looked up from the unappealing breakfast and saw Ronny heading his way.

"Mind if I join you, Colonel?"

"Please, do," Mark replied. "So, we're good with that plan we discussed?"

"Sir, I don't know. I don't want to get into any trouble I can't get out of."

Mark put his hand on Ronny's shoulder and bored into him with his kind and persuasive eyes. "Son, I wouldn't want to risk putting you in harm's way. I just thought I might be able to help you out. Nothing more. If you're uncomfortable, that's it. We'll drop it."

"No. I mean. Yes, sir. Okay, you can help me. My cousin's coming to get me. I'll make like I forgot something, and we'll pass by during the smoke break. Like we talked about."

Mark gave the young Marine a reassuring look and nodded his head. When Ronny was looking around uncomfortably, Mark looked closely at his hairline and saw no visible scars. There was nothing to indicate the presence of an implant.

"Everything's going to turn out just fine," Mark said. "Just one more favor."

"What's that, sir?"

"How many packs of cigarettes did you pick up yesterday?"

"Three. Why?"

"Marlboro's?"

"Same as always."

The entire time they were sitting, eating and talking, the broadcast news droned on but didn't include a single reference to Iran, the UCAV or Natanz. Mark thought that was interesting since there were usually follow-ups, especially to stories with the magnitude of destruction that took place at the Natanz facility.

"Come on, let's get rid of these trays," Mark said to Ronny. "I've got something for you since you'll be leaving today. A memento."

After they dropped their breakfast trays on the rack in the corridor, Mark stopped by his room and picked up the small, wooden box he'd been using to hold his shaving gear. It had been delivered along with other toiletries and uniform items that were retrieved from his quarters at Fort Meyer.

"You can empty those three packs of cigs and store them in this," he said, handing the box over to Ronny.

"That isn't necessary, sir. Really, I'll just go through 'em so fast anyway. It's just as easy to carry a pack on me."

"I insist. Just take it and bring me back the empty packs with the foil okay," Mark said.

"Aye, sir," said Ronny, without further questions.

Mark patted him on the shoulder as he left.

***

A DANGEROUS ELEMENT

DTG 051015z1211
Classification// TS/SCI: MV-ULTRA/ Eyes Only

//FM: H. Smith/Field Ops/CIA//
//TO: R. Wormwood/Deputy Director/Mid-East Field
Desk//Director SpecWar DARPA
//SUBJ: TARGET STATUS UPDATE//

A. BETHESDA NAVAL HOSPITAL (WARD 8)
1. Surveillance team in place. No change in target/Colonel
Reynolds behavior, though he's been observed interacting with
control subject, Clark. Casual encounters likely due to sharing of
cigarettes.
2. Control subject - Lance Corporal Clark - Scheduled for release
today and unaware of discharge from Marine Corps. Will continue
to monitor.

//END OF MSG//

Mark anticipated the orderly's entry to the dayroom and looked forward to the morning smoke break, not for the cigarette, but for other reasons. Since Marine Corporal Ronny Clark had been discharged, it was time for Mark to execute his escape plan. He hoped this would be his last time trekking from the psych ward through the medical facility, down to the dreary platform next to the parking garage.

Mark followed the orderly and her three charges to the "sharps" room, where they all laced up their boots before departing the ward.

"Looks cold out there," Mark said, eying the orderly. "Glad I brought my stocking cap and gloves. I don't know your Navy regs, but in the Air Force, uniform of the day has provisions for cold weather."

"Whatever suits you, Colonel. If it weren't for these bad habits…," Mark noted her sarcasm and let it go, "…we wouldn't need to dress up for the weather at all."

"Think of it as a breath of fresh air, young lady. We could all use a bit more of it after spending so much time in this depressing sanitary environment with all the uncomfortable furniture. Ever ask yourself why there isn't a single comfortable place to sit and read a book in the ward?"

"Mine is not to wonder why. Mine is but to do or die," she replied.

Mark gave her a look of approval. He noticed the other three patients standing at the door with their smokes in hand and ready to go. "Okay, then, I'm ready. Let's go," she said.

On the bottom floor, just before the three of them exited the glass double doors, Mark pulled out his black, woolen stocking cap. With his other hand, he reached into his pocket and grabbed the neatly folded foil cigarette wraps. He palmed them in his left hand, placing them over the incision behind his left ear and deftly slipping the stocking cap down over the area to hold it in place.

***

LAMB

TOP SECRET/SCI: MV-ULTRA
DTG 081855z1211
Classification// TS/SCI: MV-ULTRA/ Eyes Only

Subj: Sitrep
1. Surveillance in place. Target/Colonel Reynolds not in view yet.
Confirming Lance Corporal Clark's departure earlier today.

//END OF MSG//

TOP SECRET/SCI: MV-ULTRA
Handle VIA EYES ONLY - DESTROY IMMEDIATLY AFTER
READING

***

When the others began their individual rituals, Mark walked over to the orderly as she was tearing off a match from the matchbook she was holding.

"I thought young people all used lighters these days," he said. He knew he was interrupting her moment of peace, and hoped it meant she would agree with his request.

"Guess I'm just an old-fashioned girl, Colonel." Her tone confirmed her annoyance.

Once he had her attention, he shuffled his feet and glanced toward the ground. "I'm afraid I didn't plan this little expedition very well," Mark said. "I need to go back in and use the little boy's. For an old guy like me, things just aren't what they used to be."

She gave him a sideways glance. "You're supposed to be escorted," she said with conviction.

He raised his voice slightly, "You're afraid I'll pull my shoe laces out and try to hang myself?" He intended to sound sarcastic, but he kept it friendly. "Come on, there's a john just inside the doors," he said, tipping his head in that direction. "I'll only be a minute. I still want to smoke this before we have to go back in." He showed her his unlit cigarette.

"If I get into trouble for this, you'll pay, sir. I mean that. I'm not looking, so you'd better get your stuff movin' and be back out

here with that ciggie going before I get halfway through mine."
She sighed and jerked her thumb toward the door. "Now, hurry up
before I change my mind."

***

A DANGEROUS ELEMENT

DTG 081905z1211
Classification// TS/SCI: MV-ULTRA/ Eyes Only

Subj: Sitrep update
1. Ward patients observed taking smoke break as scheduled.
Target/Reynolds observed stationary at bldg doorway via tracking
device. Still no visual contact.

//END OF MSG//

Colonel Mark Reynolds would never be back. He never wanted to see the inside of a psych ward again. Not this one with the broken suicidal soldiers suffering from post-traumatic stress or the Ronny Clarks of the world who fell victim to the evils of the game. Colonel Reynolds had become too familiar with the unintended consequences of secret wars or otherwise. Never again.

Chapter 3

Nine Years Earlier
3 March 2002 - Bagram, Afghanistan

Captain Mark "Coolhand" Reynolds sat in the briefing room. He scanned the aluminum supports of the portable headquarters up to the decorative "455" printed above the portable building that was the Headquarters for the 455th Expeditionary Fighter Wing. Coolhand and his wingmen had just arrived from Al-Jabar, Kuwait, where they'd recently been deployed. He was among three of the other four-ship flight lead pilots, and with them were their wingmen. Together, they made up the 74th Fighter Squadron flying the A-10 Warthog used for close air support.

There was a low murmur in the room, as low as it could be considering where they'd just been. Coolhand looked around the room at his squadron mates and was pleased to know that he had one of the best groups of wingmen a flight lead could hope for.

His number two, Captain Tom "Two-Tone" Masterson, was a man he knew he could count on since they'd flown together at fighter lead-in training at Moody AFB. Call it some kind of fighter pilot telepathy, but the two rarely had to speak with one another when it involved aerial tactics.

Lieutenant Randy "Snake" Wormwood was Coolhand's second element lead, in number three. He was what pilots referred to as a fast burner. Always working the angles to improve his political position and getting all the good deal deployments. Coolhand recalled his days during primary jet training when Snake managed to come out smelling like a rose under the worst of circumstances.

Now that everyone was rounded up in Afghanistan to take care of America's business, Coolhand was willing to overlook Snake's self-servitude. As long as Snake kept up his reputation on the bombing and strafing range, Coolhand wasn't about to complain. To date, no other pilot was as consistent or as accurate as Snake was with the Gatling gun that poked from the nose of his Warthog.

If Coolhand's flight had a weakness, it was his "blue four." Typically the newest guy in the squadron would be assigned to a seasoned and competent lead, so it wasn't unreasonable for Coolhand to have the newest addition to the "Flying Tigers" in his crew. 1st Lieutenant, Billy "Bad Boy" Banyon, was a big guy with monster-sized hands. He played corner back on the USAF Academy's football team before graduating top of his class from Undergraduate Pilot Training at Vance Air Force Base, Oklahoma. Coolhand didn't see any inherent weakness from Bad Boy other than his inexperience.

When the door to the briefing room opened and Lt. Colonel Marty "Martian" Morrow stepped up on the small stage at the front of the room, everyone rose to attention and the room went immediately silent.

None of the members of the 74th ever called their squadron commander "Martian" to his face. They all referred to him as "Sir." He stood exactly five feet and five inches tall and had the appearance of an unshaven and balding aviator who'd seen his share of combat. Mark and all the pilots in his squadron respected him, not because of the decorations he wore on the dress uniform that remained in a closet back in The States either.

Mark recalled hearing that Morrow was awarded two Distinguished Flying Crosses in Desert Storm and another from action over Kosovo. But it was the Silver Star with the "V" the pilots of the Flying Tigers noticed when they looked at the official photo of their commander hanging in the hall of their squadron back home at Pope Air Force Base in North Carolina. Lt. Colonel Morrow never talked about his former exploits as a line pilot, and on the walls of his office at Pope, there was a distinct absence of

"I love me" paraphernalia. The pictures and mementos in his office were all of his family and relatives.

"Gentlemen," said the commander. "Welcome to Bagram, our new home. For how long, I don't know. Consider your arrival flights your local area orientation. Tomorrow will be the real deal. Briefing will be at 0500. I suggest everyone get some rest. That will be all."

Everyone in the room came to attention as their commander departed. When the door shut, the place erupted into a cacophony of raised voices.

"Anyone know where we'll be headed?" asked one pilot.

From another, "I wonder if they've got Triple - A waiting for us."

A redhead with freckles from another flight crew announced, "I don't give a shit if there is Anti-Aircraft-Artillery where we're headed, as long as we get to blow stuff up and fire the gun. That should do it for me. Nuff said." Coolhand and his wingmen watched the other pilots grab their kneeboards before heading out the door.

Coolhand was happy that his wingmen didn't need to be told to stick around. They gathered to him naturally, as one unit. "Guys. Just one thing before we turn in. I want Bad Boy flying my wing tomorrow."

Snake jerked his head around towards his flight lead as if he'd been slapped. Anticipating the protest, Coolhand pre-empted, "Snake, nothing on you buddy. You and Two-Tone won't have to think as hard this first time out. I want Bad Boy's first taste of combat to be delicious enough for him to be eager for another meal. Alright, let's get some chow and shuteye. It's gonna feel pretty early come morning."

The morning briefing definitely felt too soon. Mark knew that none of the Tigers of the 74th would complain, though. It was an unwritten rule that you showed up to briefing revved and ready, regardless of the amount of sleep you got.

"Okay, fellas, the mission brief seemed pretty straightforward," Coolhand began.

He initiated the flight briefing by synchronizing their watches, known to all pilots as a "time hack." Bad Boy already had the white board filled out with all the 'by-the-book' admin items and basic flight profile responsibilities. After briefing the emergency and contingency procedures, Coolhand went over the specific operational mission details, starting with the primary and secondary targets.

"As mentioned in this morning's brief, our targets are in the Khost and Paktia provinces. The area is in the southeast end of the Shah-e-Kot Valley. The entire area is mountainous. In particular, the Arma Mountains southeast of Zormat could be tricky. Two days ago there were reports of mobile ZSU 23s hidden in there."

"Triple-A. Fuckin' great," Snake said under his breath.

Coolhand ignored the comment, turning his attention to the white board. He drew with a different color for each of the three options, then went over the details of each. Once airborne, he wanted the flexibility to adjust mission objectives using brevity codes, rather than lengthy discussions.

Using an orange dry erase, Coolhand circled a region on the plastic-covered chart of the area that hung beside the briefing board.

"Comms haven't been too reliable out there. We'll have inter-plane, but only in the clear. So, before you key that mic, be thinking about our operational security. We'll keep the encrypted freqs up as much as possible for mission updates from AOC — that way nobody will key up unless it's critical. Stick to the contract, and everyone comes home with targets destroyed."

When he paused, his crew shifted their attention back to the whiteboard to copy the mission data points onto the line-up cards clipped to their knee boards. He gave them a minute to finish taking their notes.

"Last order of business will be tanker support. The ARCO tanker orbit will be to the South. We shouldn't need extra gas for this one, but if anyone is bumping joker in the box or suspects battle damage, I want a head's up to coordinate the refueling before recovering to base. Questions?" Mark didn't expect any from this disciplined group. "Good. Let's saddle up."

As they gathered their line-up cards and kneeboards and headed to the chute shop, Mark clapped Bad Boy on the shoulder. The younger pilot didn't seem the least bit nervous. He admired this trait in his wingmen.

"You up for this?" he asked.

"I was born for it, sir," he said. "You lead, I'll follow." Then, he grinned and added, "Thanks for askin', sir."

Coolhand always felt good strapping the hog to his back. It was a powerful addition to his own five-foot, eleven inch frame. He thought the designers at Fairchild built the plane especially for him. He was able to go through his pre-flight checks with seamless precision without having to lean or bend his body. Every switch and button on the front and side panels was perfectly matched for his reach. Even the buttons and toggles on the throttle fit perfectly into his gloved hand.

After engine start, and with his pre-taxi checks complete, Coolhand made a visual check of the other members in his flight. They were ready to go. He keyed the mic on ground freq.

"Gunfighter Check," he said.

"Two,"

"Three,"

"Four," came the responses in cadence through the headphones.

"Ground, Gunfighter Zero Eight. Flight of four. Ridge Fire 3, Taxi with Uniform."

"Gunfighter Zero Eight. Taxi Runway 21 winds three-zero-zero at five altimeter three-zero-zero-four."

Coolhand acknowledged the instructions with ground and worked his flight out to the armament pad. Just prior to requesting take-off clearance, a ground crew performed the final inspections and pulled the safety pins from the bombs slung beneath the wings of all four aircraft.

"Tower Gunfigher, Zero Eight with four ready for take off."

"Gunfigher Zero Eight. You're cleared for Ridge Fire 3-East Transition. Cleared takeoff. Contact departure."

"Roger. Cleared take-off. Gunfighters, push Gold Two."

"Two, Three, Four," was the monotone response Coolhand heard in his headset. He and his wingmen were all on the same page.

Captain Mark "Coolhand" Reynolds was back in his element. He gave his pilots a series of hand signals directing them to push their power to the max with brakes set for a final check of the engines. Coolhand could feel the aircraft's powerful twin turbo-fans and noted the thumbs up from his wingmen. He tapped his helmet to get their attention before giving them an exaggerated head nod indicating brake release. He and Bad Boy were in the air with wheels in the well just as the second element released their brakes. Snake and Two-Tone were off the runway and into the air with the efficiency of a well-oiled machine. Looking over his left shoulder, Coolhand could see the steady pace of Snake and Two-Tone coming up for the rejoin. He looked over to his right where Bad Boy was welded in position three feet off his wingtip. All four aircraft joined up and checked in on departure frequency, then they made their turn to the southeast.

Once they were joined up in fingertip, the next order of business included visual inspections and a fuel check. With the chores completed, Coolhand spread his wingmen into a tactical formation for the trip to the target area.

Coolhand could feel his pulse increase slightly as he and his flight entered "the box," the zone set up for combat operations. Once there, Coolhand gave the signal for weapons checks. He knew the other Warthog pilots got their own special thrill from toggling off the safety switches and squeezing the trigger on the stick. The single pull on the trigger fires 3900 rounds of 30 millimeter hard point every minute. The short burst reminded Coolhand of the awesome firepower living within his aircraft.

Chapter 4

4 March 2002 -
"The Box" Khost Province Afghanistan

The fluid nature of Gunfighter flight's mission made it possible to provide close air support for the extraction of some ground troops trapped in the hills near Takur Ghar Peak. The night before, a Marine CH 47 callsign Mako 30 crashed in the vicinity. Captain "Coolhand" Reynolds and his Gunfighters were well on their way to protect the extraction zone from mobile mortar and machine gun emplacements reported to be operated by Taliban.

After their weapons check, Coolhand signaled the formation to tighten. He then passed a hand signal to the formation to "go green" on the encrypted Ultra High Frequency channel – their most secure com line.

When Coolhand keyed up, he heard the telltale pre-amble

chirp before transmitting instructions to his wingmen.

"Gunfighter."

The three responses were synchronized perfectly, each pilot waited for the pre-amble before chiming in,

"Beep-beep Two, beep-beep Three, beep-beep Four."

"Disco - Gunfighter Zero Eight." Coolhand waited before attempting another contact with the AWACs.

"Nothing heard, Gunfighters, Go Gold Three." Coolhand wanted his wingmen on an operable frequency where they would have some chance of gaining information on the targets. After everyone was checked in, he attempted contact with the Air Operations Center.

A weak and broken signal came back from the AOC, "Gunfighter Zero Eight, this is King Pen …we hear you, but can't…remain on frequency, be advised…" The line went silent again.

Coolhand looked over his left shoulder at Bad Boy for any indication of receiving the transmission from AOC. He got back a negative headshake. To his right, he got the same from Snake. They needed to get back into a tactical formation.

"Gunfighters - Execute Option One."

The dust from one of the extraction helicopters made locating the first objective easy. Coolhand set up his flight in a figure eight pattern, giving each Warthog pilot a piece of the perimeter to sanitize. Option One required each of them to drop their Mark 82 bombs, then remain on the ready with the 30 mm cannon's controls to watch for pop-ups. It was simple and effective.

Coolhand felt his pulse pump and his heart rate increase as he rolled into a semi-inverted pitch back maneuver, loading his aircraft to five times the force of gravity, instantly compressing his body. The effects were short-lived as Coolhand rolled out in a steep, wing-level dive heading straight for his target. He could see the ground tracer being fired in the direction of Mako-30's crash site and aligned the reticle in the head up display over his target. When he hit the right altitude and dive angle, Coolhand pickled off his two Mark 82's and then started to pull up.

The rapid onset of Gs once again loaded up his wings. His G-suit inflated, squeezing his thighs and torso. Reflexively, he tensed his muscles and rapidly exhaled, drawing short breaths at intervals to offset the pressure. His helmeted head, now seven times its normal weight, pressed down against his neck and shoulders. He performed a quick, tight roll and looked back over his right shoulder to see the bombs hit their mark.

He arrested any further altitude gain by letting his arc end with him inverted at the top. He was relieved when he saw Bad Boy over his left shoulder unloading a burst from his hog's cannon, causing secondary explosions from a nearby ammo dump. And in the seconds it took Coolhand to take a quick glance at his altitude,

Bad Boy was already pulling up onto a rejoin line with him.

All seemed to be going well for the pilots of Gunfighter flight. When the remaining CH-47 Chinook was airborne and safely leaving the extraction zone, Coolhand had the other two wingmen reformed and maneuvering for their secondary target area north of Takur Ghar.

"Gunfighters - Option Three," Coolhand transmitted over the UHF to his wingmen.

When he didn't get a response, Coolhand turned to see Snake and Two-Tone breaking away from formation. They pitched up and headed to the southeast, heading back to the targeted extraction area.

"What the fuck?" Coolhand asked himself. "Snake, you son of a bitch...never could follow instructions, could you."

Coolhand looked over at Bad Boy glued to his right wing. He crossed his wingman over to his left side with a tactical weave and looped the two-ship element back around in search of Snake and Two-Tone.

As they rolled out, Coolhand saw Snake's aircraft pitching up and rolling high and right as he came off another target. Muzzle flashes and tracer rounds raked the sky in his wake, but Snake appeared to be maneuvering away unscathed.

Coolhand worked his element around the backside of the ridge, so the Taliban guerillas wouldn't detect them while they reformed for an RTB. He could still see the tracer fire as Two-Tone came off the target. Two-Tone was already in an arcing circle for a right turning rejoin with Snake when there was a sudden explosion causing secondaries to pop off in every direction. The entire area erupted with enemy ground fire directed at Two-Tone's hog.

"Gunfighters Check," Coolhand called. When two of his three wingmen checked in, he transmitted the following, "Rejoin left, Angels -Twelve, One Eight-Zero."

Coolhand checked to see Bad Boy crossing inside on his left like he was supposed to. He was beginning to really like flying with the younger pilot. Standard procedure didn't seem to register well with Snake, and that made him a liability.

As they headed back to the northwest, he saw Snake up on the horizon belly-up toward the formation on an easy rejoin line. There was no sign of Two-Tone.

Coolhand could feel the sweat trickling down the side of his face from beneath his helmet. He reached up, unclipped his oxygen mask and lifted his visor to quickly wipe the moisture with the back of his gloved hand before refastening his mask.

"Gunfighter Two, I need you to get a tally on Two-Tone."

"Two," Bad Boy transmitted that he understood Coolhand's instructions.

When Snake finally closed the gap and joined the right side of their formation, Coolhand spotted several fuel leaks coming from Snake's right wing and aft fuselage.

"Gunfighter Two. Any sign of Two-Tone?"

"No Joy," Bad Boy said over the UHF.

Shit. Twenty seconds ago, he had four healthy birds. Now, he had one missing and one sick.

"Snake. State your fuel."

"Gunfighter Three is Bingo."

Coolhand checked his own fuel state. He had at least thirty more minutes of fuel for loitering before reaching Joker. He could make another pass before returning to base.

"Gunfighter Three, take Two with you and immediately RTB. You're leaking fuel, and it looks like you'll need ARCO support before you can recover. How copy?"

"Three Copies."

"Gunfighter Three, you're cleared off. Contact ARCO for coordination and relay that Gunfighter Four is missing. I'm sticking around to reconnoiter and will remain on station for Search and Rescue."

"Three copies. Four check state."

"Four's Joker plus eight hundred."

"Copy. Push 'Copper Six.'"

The UHF went quiet. Coolhand watched as the second element climbed. They'd need to conserve fuel in order to make it to the tanker. Bad Boy and Snake's wounded bird disappeared in short order.

Coolhand returned to the area above the high plateau where he last saw Two-Tone. He tried to recall the direction of the tracer fire, but it had happened too fast.

"Kingpin, Gunfighter Zero Eight?" he called in the blind. Nothing. *Shit*, Coolhand thought, *he must be too low for contact.*

He took one more trip over the area, following in the direction he guessed Two-Tone might have turned after pulling off the target. He was looking for any sign of a crash site or a chute. Still nothing.

He checked his fuel state. The low altitude was burning up his reserves, in spite of the efficiency of his hog's pair of GE TF34 turbo fan engines. He climbed upward to above four thousand feet, hoping he'd have enough gas for another survey of the area and maybe even get lucky enough to pick-up Kingpin on the UHF to direct some SAR support for Two-Tone.

At fifteen thousand MSL, he was clear of terrain by several thousand feet in all directions. He was glad to hear some chatter on Kingpin's freq. It sounded like Snake at least came through to coordinate the Search and Rescue. Although, it seemed more likely that Bad Boy was the one making sure Two-Tone was going to be looked after.

"Kingpin, Gunfighter Zero Eight," Coolhand called. The SAR

effort would need updated coordinates on Gunfighter Zero Eight Dash 4, so he passed them and reported he was Bingo and RTB.

En route back to Bagram, Coolhand heard Grapple Two-Three reporting there was heavy ground fire in the vicinity of the coordinates Coolhand provided and that they didn't get a beacon or hear any ground transmissions, so they were aborting. Coolhand couldn't blame them. One downed aircraft was enough for one day.

Snake and Bad Boy would already be on deck by the time he entered the pattern. He also knew there'd be some explaining to do. He had no idea what he was going to say to Lieutenant Colonel Morrow after the debrief, but knew he'd be on the carpet in front of the squadron commander. He just hoped Snake hadn't gotten to him first.

When he arrived at debrief, Snake and Bad Boy were waiting for him. Bad Boy looked no worse for wear, but Coolhand could tell he was appropriately concealing the sort of shit-eating-grin a first-timer normally sported after returning from combat unscathed. Coolhand was proud to watch as the fledgling pilot focused his comments on providing as much information as possible that might help SAR locate their wingman.

As anticipated, the "Martian" was standing in the corridor when they emerged from debrief. Lieutenant Colonel Morrow eyed Coolhand with some degree of compassion.

"Captain Reynolds, a word in my office please." He held an open hand in the direction of his office.

Coolhand obediently led the way.

"Take a seat, Mark," the commander said. He shut the door behind him and came around to take his own chair behind his desk. Lieutenant Colonel Morrow didn't say anything to Mark right away. He was gauging whether the seasoned flight lead would make the mistake of jumping in with an excuse disguised as an explanation for the mission fuck-up. Mark reached up and raked his fingers through his brush cut, then Morrow spoke with the measured words of a commander who'd seen his share of combat and the fog of confusion that often accompanies an aerial engagement gone wrong.

"During Desert Storm, when one of my squadron mates pulled off-target low over a column of vehicles heading north out of Kuwait City, I saw the plane roll on its back and couldn't see a chute. Nobody heard a beacon either. When we were all in debrief, we were pretty sure we'd seen the last of Captain Stan Daley. Two and a half months later, Stan was released from an Iraqi detention facility along with the other POWs. You should have seen him. We thought we'd never see him again." The commander paused and bore a look into Mark's eyes, then said, "You catch my drift, Mark?"

"Yes, sir."

"What happened out there?"

"Did Snake talk to you yet?"

"It doesn't matter what Snake might or might not have said. You were flight lead, and I want to know the pertinent details," Morrow demanded.

Mark wasn't one to dime out his wingmen, regardless of whether he thought Snake disobeyed his commands.

"Sir, everything was routine. There was no contact with AWAC's support." Mark paused, trying to line up the chronology of the mission anomalies as they occurred.

"Figures," Morrow said. "Go on."

"We checked in with Kingpin but lost them entirely at about the time we entered the box to set up support cover for Mako's extraction."

"Comms have been a problem in that area for everyone since air ops started. What else can you tell me about it?"

"Nothing, sir. Deader than a doornail even after we lost track of Two-Tone. What pisses me off is that the guys driving the Predator Drones around can do their job from all the way back in the states and have solid comms the entire time. One lousy drone with two little Hellfires and they get all the good comm. I don't get it."

Mark sat back in his chair, trying to keep his frustration in check.

"They've got Ku Sat links. Solid as stone. We're going to have to come up with something better, or we're going to be dealing with more missions like the Mako pick up." Morrow rose from his chair and moved out from behind his desk.

Mark stood to attention while his commander rose, then stood by to be excused. Morrow opened the door for Mark and looked him in the eye.

"Coolhand, you'd better get some chow and some rest. If I can't get you another wingman, I'll have the Opso frag you for a two-ship. We're putting everyone who isn't sick or broken in the air again tomorrow."

When Mark left the commander's office, he wanted nothing more than to track down Snake and punch his lights out. He was damn sure he didn't want his undisciplined ass on any more Gunfighter missions. He hoped he'd be fragged for a two-ship in the morning, so he could take Bad Boy along with him again. Green as he might be, young Billy Banyon was loyal and could fly the shit out of his Hog.

CHAPTER 5

Late Summer 2003 - Isfahan, Iran

When he heard the crack of the starting gun, Reza felt the familiar surge of adrenalin rush into every muscle of his being. He was twenty meters beyond the spot in the road where he'd put his toe on the line at the start of the first ten-kilometer competition he'd entered in many years. He knew already that he was running faster than the pace he originally set for himself. Controlling his excitement and managing his energy state was something he'd have to do within the first kilometer or he'd defeat his own strategy.

Earlier that week, Dr. Farrouk "Reza" Khedem decided to enter a ten-kilometer event sponsored by a group of runners from his alma mater at the University of Isfahan. The weather was perfect for a running event, especially since the start time was in the early morning before the heat of the day set in. Reza drove to the event in the Peugeot 405 that his father handed down to him when he finished grad school.

He arrived at the specified location. He was aware that he arrived well before the scheduled start time but didn't expect the place to look so deserted. Reza wasn't sure if he'd mixed up the time or date of the event. He dug around in his duffle to look again the copy of the flyer announcing the details of the event. *Yes*, he thought, *this is the right place*. He looked again at his beat up Casio, checking the time. Just when he was about to give up and head back to Natanz, two young men driving a pick-up arrived and quickly unloaded a folding table and several boxes from the truck's cargo area. Within twenty minutes, the entire area was transformed as runners began to show up. Reza was exited. In an effort to control the anticipation of competing, he warmed up with some of the other runners until the familiar buzz of activity came to a crescendo when the gun was fired.

Crossing the first kilometer marker, Reza glanced at his watch. Through the crazed crystal, he could barely make out the numbers, which read three minutes and twenty seconds. "Gotta slow down," he said to himself. It was a good split for the later stages of the race, but right now he knew he'd need to keep his speed in check, or risk running slower near the end. Other runners were passing him and he reminded himself he'd been in this same situation back in the days when he used to compete regularly. "I'll see them later down the road, when I reel them in one by one," he said to himself.

As he approached the second kilometer marker, he glanced again at his watch. In spite of exerting himself, he was relaxed and he grinned at the realization that he'd gained control of his pace. He was on autopilot now, so he allowed his mind to wander. He didn't think of himself as a typical Iranian scientist and engineer and wasn't about to bend to every will and desire of a government that paid for his education. "I never want to be a robot." It was a mantra Reza had been telling himself since his college days. Since then, he did what was expected of him, at the same time priding himself in his closely guarded individuality.

Believing he could make the entire distance without hydrating himself, he skipped the water stop at the four kilometer mark. It was only his self-discipline that kept him from speeding up after he saw a few of the other runners who grabbed cups of water from the volunteers had passed him again. "I'm sticking to the plan," he whispered to himself under his own steady breathing. It reminded him of earlier times in his life. His one pleasure was running.

His love for the sport grew when he was an exchange student in France studying physics at University of Paris-Sud. He thought how wonderful it would have been if he didn't have to study or work. He'd be able to train. Maybe even travel to Boulder, Colorado in the United States to train, like the Kenyan and Australian runners.

After he completed his first marathon in 2:48:20, he thought that with dedicated training he could own the national record and maybe even compete in the Olympics. His countryman, Hossein Behdouj, set Iran's record in a marathon run in Mashad the year before. At that point, Reza realized he wasn't getting any younger and Behjouj's 2:28:23 was going to be out of reach for him.

Reza soon discovered that long-distance running was just an escape for him. Preserving his sanity through a disciplined fitness regimen provided him with a daily distraction and sense of wellbeing. Additionally, the daily dose of endorphins fueled his creative mind. It enabled him to imagine an Iran without pollution. Tehran could become a city like Boulder, Colorado, though much larger. He envisioned the suburbs of northern Tehran becoming a haven for athletes from all over his country. He also imagined that every family could have access to the Internet and the learning possibilities that came with universal education.

The six kilometer marker blew by and he checked his watch, confirming he was right on schedule for running the race using the strategy he'd planned for. It was time for him to speed up. A little at a time, just a bit faster for each of the four kilometers remaining, and the negative splits would have him passing the other runners ahead that he could tell were running out of energy. Reza still felt fresh and stepped up his pace, reeling in the first of those other runners out ahead that he knew he could beat.

He dove back into the recesses of his mind to avoid thinking about the strain of the increased pace. He recalled some of the events that brought him to this point. After he completed his degree, he was recruited by the Ministry of Science, Research and Technology in his country's capital to assist with the planning and design of a nuclear enrichment facility. The memory took him back to the morning in Tehran when he woke early as he'd been doing since his school days. He took in a deep breath before stretching out his Achilles and loosening his shoulders. He could taste the stale air even though it was too early for the smog to accumulate, thickening it all the more.

Reza wasn't passionate about his work, but he knew he was good at it and understood the complexities of nuclear enrichment. He had a vision that one day his beloved Tehran would no longer suffer from the air pollution. The filthy air was so bad that it forced him to take his morning runs in the earliest hours before the roads were choked with automobiles, buses, and diesel trucks.

He remembered the first time he met his lovely wife, Termeh. Their marraige was arranged for them by their affluent families, both from the Valenjak neighborhood in the northern section of Tehran. On their first encounter, Termeh made a comment about him being so fit and smart, not like the other men her parents arranged for her to meet, she told him.

Reza toiled over how to tell Termeh they would be leaving

Tehran. By the time he returned to the foyer of their modern apartment complex, Reza was convinced that the eloquent speech he'd prepared would make Termeh proud of him. He was sure that when he told her of his promotion to Plant and Facilities Director at Natanz, she'd be thrilled.

"It will mean moving there at the end of summer," he said to his wife as he held her gently at arm's length.

He was taken aback by her reaction. He reached for her as she was pushing away, and was startled by her tone of voice when she burst out, "I'm to give up my work? Just what am I to do in Natanz, Reza, tell me. That place is in the middle of nowhere," she protested.

"We can live in Isfahan. I'll commute. It isn't as if I actually have a choice in this matter, Termeh. What do you think would happen if I refused?" Reza reasoned.

"You go then. I understand, but I'm staying in Tehran. The desert is so primitive. I'm a doctor and I have a growing practice. It would be a waste to abandon all my work, and for what, a few extra Rial each month for you while I wither in the courtyard waiting for you to return from work each evening?"

Reza just stood and watched Termeh turn away from him. She grabbed her satchel containing the medical journals she reserved for reviewing while riding the bus to her office each morning. She pulled up the hood of the black chadar to cover her auburn hair and left him standing in the foyer still sweating from his morning run.

Reza packed his belongings and on his own, he made his way to Natanz. The Ministry of Science, Research and Technology provided him with living quarters. The small studio appartment was located in a compound adjacent to a concrete and steel structure under construction several miles from the nearest inhabitants of Natanz.

Reza lived alone as did many of the other scientists and engineers residing there during the week. Each Friday after his morning run, he drove back to Tehran to spend the weekend with Termeh. It was a livable arrangement.

Reza snapped back into the reality of the moment as he approached the final water stop with only two kilometers remaining in the race. He was beginning to feel the heat and figured it was because he'd been steadily increasing his speed. He'd passed a group of runners and didn't see anyone else immediately ahead of him, so he grabbed a water cup from one of the volunteers and crushed the top of it so no water would spill out. He continued to run at only a slightly slower pace, taking sips over the next hundred meters or so. After he pitched the empty cup to the side of the road, he felt energized.

Reza was keenly aware of his leg speed and the rhythm of his pace. He didn't expect to hear the footfalls of another runner as he continued to increase his pace toward the finish. He noticed the other runner was close to his age but was breathing much harder, having caught up with only a half a kilometer to go.

The other runner kept increasing his speed. Reza thought he could sprint to the finish, so he accelerated to a pace he thought he could maintain all the way to the end. He rapidly went into oxygen debt but didn't let up as he heard the footfalls of the other runner always present and challenging him for a better finishing position.

The finish was the most dramatic Reza had ever experienced. He nearly collapsed after striding across the line at the end. He was breathing so hard he wasn't able to open his eyes or focus for at least a half a minute or so. It was a tap on the shoulder that brought him back to consciousness. The other runner stood alongside him, also breathing hard.

"Congratulations," he said. "My name is Heydar. You really gave me a run. I wanted to catch you so badly I didn't realize I'd used up all my reserves until the last ten meters. No matter, though, today my time was a personal best. I thank you for helping me achieve it."

Reza looked at his ancient Casio runner's watch. It was still running. He didn't know what his time was. "Pleased to meet you, Heydar, I'm Reza. Forgive me that I ask, but my watch, I forgot to press the button and it still runs. What was your time?"

"Thirty-four minutes and twenty-eight seconds," Heydar told

him.

Reza reached out with his arm and shook Heydar's already extended hand. "It is a personal best for me as well. I don't know that I've ever run so fast. I suspect my time was only a second ahead of yours."

"No, it had to be more. You were well through the finish line before I even entered the final chute. Are you from around here?" he asked Reza.

"No. Up the road at the engineer's compound."

"Oh, so you aren't with the university then?" Heydar asked.

"Well, yes and no. I graduated from here several years ago but I work for the government in Natanz now," Reza replied.

"I'd have figured you for one of the new university professors since I've never seen you around. I am a graduate student. I love running in Isfahan. Too bad you aren't available during the week. We could do track workouts together."

"You do track workouts?" Reza asked as the two runners proceeded to a table where they retrieved some energy drinks and bananas.

"No, sorry. I imagine that I would do track workouts if I had a compatible training partner. I've tried on my own, but it's not fun running on the track doing repeat quarters against a clock. Not alone anyway. When I was an undergraduate student in Tehran, I trained with other runners and back then I did track workouts."

"I've never trained on the track," said Reza.

"You'd be amazed at what it can do to improve your speed. Especially in the Ten Kilometer," Heydar told him, still elated by the possibility of achieving an even faster time with some additional training.

Reza thought about it for a few moments, doing a mental calculation of how long it would take to drive both directions from Natanz and squeeze in a workout. "I can meet you here on Thursday evenings if you'd like to train together," Reza offered.

"Really? That would be great. Next week then, say six thirty? We could 'carbo load' after. You know, eat some food, get to know each other better?"

The two runners shook hands and agreed to meet the following Thursday. Both of them checked in with the race organizers before heading off in separate directions. Later that week, he read in the sports section university's gazette that he'd placed third in his age group for 34-39 year old male runners.

CHAPTER 6

September 2004 - Langley Air Force Base Virginia

Major Mark Reynolds hated the idea of his new staff job at Air Combat Command. He knew he'd like the people well enough. The leadership seemed solid to him and his Division Chief reminded him of his former Squadron Commander, Lieutenant Colonel Morrow, only taller.

"You know why you're here don't you, Major?" Colonel Greg "Sam" Spade asked.

Mark stood before the Colonel in an office with large windows facing the brick headquarters building across the street that housed the Commander of Air Combat Command, General Keith, often referred to as COMACC. Mark could see that Sam thought the world of his commander. He sensed that his new boss was interested in the knowledge and experience he gained through his recent combat experience. He also knew that guys like Sam Spade were usually only interested in what it might take to be wearing a star or two of their own.

"You're our one and only Hog expert with combat experience. Aside from the airframe's 'life extension program,' COMACC is going to authorize some priority program money to fix the communication problems that seem to be plaguing our pilots operating in Afghanistan. I heard you thought there might be an easy solution. Can you give me an overview?" the colonel asked.

Mark was a little surprised. In his experience, his first day's meeting with the new boss usually included a 'welcome aboard,' speech, and 'how is it going as far as settling in?' Instead, Spade wanted him to get to work right away.

The move to Langley didn't go as he'd planned. It was only two weeks earlier that his wife, Anne, gave him the ultimatum before he drove off from their home in Valdosta Georgia. "If we're going to pack up and move one more time," she'd said, "I'm taking the girls with me back to Denver. You've been like a ghost even when you're home. Your own daughters don't even know who you are anymore, and I'm getting fed up."

He didn't think Anne sounded angry when she spoke to him. He actually felt sympathetic. He sensed a distance growing between them following his two tours to Afghanistan. She never complained about his spending more and more time at work either, causing him to wonder if there was another man in her life, but he knew not to ask.

"Anne, I'm sorry. It's all my fault. You do what you've got to do. I don't blame you. Neither of us ever liked the South anyway. I know you and the girls would enjoy Virginia, though. If you want to go back to Colorado I won't stand in your way, but I wish you'd think about joining me in Virginia. There's the beach and the history. Washington D.C. is just up the road and the girls are getting to the age where they could enjoy visiting the sites. Just keep the door open to the idea," he said before setting off in his beat up Honda Civic for the long drive to Hampton Roads.

Mark saw the white board on the side wall of the colonel's office. Before explaining his proposed solution to the close air support communication problem in Afghanistan, he stood gesturing towards it and asked, "Sir, do you mind if I..?"

"Please, do. The dry erase markers are in the box on that small table," the colonel said, pointing to the markers.

Mark took a few moments to draw a diagram on the white board in three different colors. When he was done, he pointed to each of the key components, highlighting the problem as he'd experienced it. Then, he picked up the green and blue-colored markers and drew in a couple of other elements of the communications environment, showing some steep hills and valleys representing a typical operations area.

"Sir, we've had some success with the forward air control

pieces of the operation. As you know a few of our guys are imbedded with locals and have been operating as Forward Air Controllers while on horseback with a laptop and 'Iridium Sat Links.' They've had constant and persistent connectivity with the AOC, but only from exposed positions near the tops of ridges. When they seek cover, they can still link up with the Iridium birds, but then they lose contact with the supporting aircraft. Sir, we simply can't afford to lose any of these FACs to the Taliban. It would be a disaster. Furthermore…"

"No need to elaborate, Major. I've got the picture. I need to know what this easy solution is you've been pushing for."

"Right. Well, if the FACs are having success with Iridium, I thought, why can't we? It isn't like we're going to be competing with commercial customers for band width either. When Motorola developed the constellation of satellites supporting the program, they had no way of knowing that the network of towers supporting cellular would outpace their program and become cheaper for the customer, so they have a bunch of underutilized balls up there. We'd just need our industry partners to come onboard and offer up use."

"What you're proposing is open and constant communications with AOC via Iridium?" the colonel asked.

"In a nut shell, yes, sir," Mark replied with some enthusiasm.

"I'm listening. Go on."

"The Hogs are already wired for ACMI pods, as are our Vipers," he explained.

Air Combat Maneuvering Instrumentation is used on the "Red Flag" range at Nellis Air Force Base in Nevada. The small, blue-colored, dart-shaped tubes are mounted on one of the aircraft pylons under the wing. They were lightweight and had their own self-contained antennas to relay telemetry data back to the Operations Center for post-mission analysis during "Red Flag" exercises.

"All we'd need to do is replace the ACMI antenna in the pod with Iridium antennas. The guts from the Iridium Sat Phone could be mounted directly in the pod and easily wired into the aircraft's interphone amplifier.

"Okay, let's go see COMACC. I want him to hear this directly from you. Just as you laid it out." Mark could see that Spade was glowing with enthusiasm by what he heard. He watched and listened while Spade picked up his phone and dialed into the Four Star's executive officer.

"Hello? Yes. We've got a briefing and tell him I believe we can do this as an advanced concept technology demo and have a solution in the field in less than a month if we can pull some strings with his contacts at Motorola," Mark waited as the colonel replaced the handset in its cradle and looked over at him.

"You think you could put a few briefing slides together to take over to COMACC in an hour?" Spade asked.

"Sir, I don't even have a desk yet, let alone a network account."

Mark knew his comment wouldn't phase Spade one bit. He stood by while the colonel got up from behind his desk. Mark saw the colonel's open-handed gesture leading his eyes toward a work station set up in a corner of the large office.

"You can use mine. I've got to go down and chat with General Glazer. Let him know we're seeing the old man across the street. I'll be back in about forty-five minutes. If you need anything, ask Janet in the front office…and I mean, if you need a lackey to help you spruce up the slides, have her round up another action officer to give you a hand," No sooner said and the colonel was out the door.

Mark didn't need any assistance with the slides. He simply recreated the diagrams he'd drawn on his new boss's white board and layered them in as animations, so that during his presentation, each idea would build on the next, telling a convincing story. He added a conclusion on a separate slide to use as backup just in case.

The concept he used to support his approach was the development of the GBU-28 Bunker Buster Glide Bomb Units dropped by a pair of F-111s near the end of Desert Storm. It took only two weeks to develop and test the concept before deploying those experimental weapons to Saudi Arabia where they were flown into Iraq and successfully dropped, destroying the hardened targets south of Bagdad. That program was a wildly successful example of an ACTD taken directly to the operational environment.

Less than an hour later, Mark clicked the "save" button with the computer's mouse and looked up when Colonel Spade entered the office.

"Major General Glazer wants us to go ahead without him. He's tied up on a call with a congressman. Are you about ready?" Spade asked.

Mark picked up the five pieces of paper printed in color and extracted a flash drive Janet provided him with earlier. "Ready as ever, sir," he said, rolling the charts in his left hand and picking up his flight cap with the other.

When they entered the glass doors at the end of the hall on the second floor, Mark and his new boss were met by a young-looking officer wearing a flight suit. Mark saw the name plate on the executive officer's desk. It read, "Lieutenant Colonel Steve Voughn." Mark followed Spade as the exec escorted the two of them into the Four Star General's office. Mark looked around and noticed the place looked like a museum or at least a shrine to combat aviation. What he didn't expect was to see just how aged and worn out the Four Star appeared to be. General Keith didn't even look up when the officers initially entered the room. "Do you have a briefing for me?" he asked.

"Yes, sir, this is Major Mark Reynolds, goes by 'Coolhand,'" Colonel Spade said.

Mark saw that General Keith's eyes looked like they were focused on the papers rolled up in Marks left hand. "Are those the charts?" he asked, pointing to Mark's papers.

"Yes, sir," Mark said, unrolling them as he approached the General's desk. "I've got a PowerPoint version that tells the story a bit better if you'd like to see it," he said.

The General rapidly sifted through the five sheets of paper Mark handed him before looking up at the younger officer, "How come I've never seen you around before, Coolhand?"

"Sir, I just arrived this morning from Moody."

The General just nodded and looked at the first chart again. "Fighter Aircraft Communications Enhancement. FACE. I like it." Then, he punched a button next to the phone on his desk and in an instant, his exec popped back into the office.

A moment later, the general issued an order to his executive officer who was poking his head through the doorway. "Stevie Ray, whatever we've got on for one o'clock in the conference room, I want you to shuffle things around and have the Vice and Major General Glazer join us. Come to think of it, I want the POLAD and the Scientific Advisor in there also."

"Let's see this briefing of yours. You can plug it into that console on the table." The General pointed to where Mark could plug in the flash stick, then he picked up a remote and a projector illuminated a screen on the back wall.

Mark plugged in the stick and the General quickly navigated to the first slide, projecting it full screen, then handed the remote to Mark.

When Mark was done, the General didn't say anything. He just nodded before looking up at the two officers, indicating the meeting was over, and then said, "See you both in the conference room at one. Oh, and Coolhand?"

"Sir?" Mark answered.

"Good job and keep your game face on," the general said in a warm, encouraging tone.

When they left, Colonel Spade clapped Mark on the shoulder. They walked across the street back to the Colonel's office. "Not bad for your first day. Showcasing a brand new idea and getting an audience with COMACC. You know this never happens. It's a first for me."

Mark didn't know what to think. He glanced at his watch and noticed there wouldn't be time for lunch before returning to the headquarters building where he'd be presenting the FACE story to the movers and shakers of Air Combat Command.

Less than an hour later, he was in a large conference room.

More elaborate than any he'd ever been in, aside from the ACMI theater at Nellis. Colonel Spade arranged so that Stevie Ray had everything all set up for him when they returned. Mark figured Spade made sure they arrived at the conference room just before the General entered so that there wouldn't be any time to get nervous about pitching the presentation. The other senior officers and officials were already seated at the table.

Mark was already standing and the others came to attention when General Keith entered. He remained standing when the General asked the others to be seated, knowing General Keith was going to introduce him and the FACE program.

The briefing went even better than it did earlier. Mark stood at the front of the room anticipating questions from at least one pessimistic observer, but the only question that came was from the Scientific Advisor, Carla Simpson.

"How soon do you think we can have something like this in the field, Major?" she asked.

"I'll answer that one, Coolhand," Major General Glazer chimed in. "I'll make a few calls this afternoon and we can have a prototype ready to test before the end of the week.

"Is that a promise 'Slip Stream?'" General Keith asked, using Glazer's nickname.

"Sir, not a promise, but based on the forethought my boy Coolhand's already put into this thing, I'm pretty confident we'll have something by then."

"Okay, Coolhand, whatever you need, get with Stevie Ray. I don't want anything to hang this up. Our guys need this capability and there's no excuse for not already having something like this out there. Thanks for your work."

When the General stood to depart, so did everyone else. The FACE program was going to become a reality for the Hog drivers in Afghanistan, and Major Mark "Coolhand" Reynolds wished he could experience it, but knew his career and his fate were now in the hands of his leaders.

CHAPTER 7

Fall 2005 - University of Isfahan

Reza felt good about the track workout he and Heydar just completed. No longer out of breath from the speed workout, he slowed into a steady jog and noticed his training partner was equally relaxed.

"If you're available at other times besides Thursday evenings, we should mix up our workouts from now on," Reza suggested.

"How will we be able to do that with your schedule?" Haydar asked.

"The Atomic Energy Organization of Iran is undergoing some re-organization and since the work I've been doing at the facility in Natanz is well underway, they've decided to temporarily move my projects closer to the research and development nuclear reactor near the Isfahan campus." Reza was grinning from ear to ear, hoping his friend would be excited.

"This is great news! Yes, of course, we'll have to compare our training schedules and maybe even enter a big race to keep things interesting," Heydar said.

Several weeks later, Reza realized he was happier than he'd been in months. He was able to convince his wife, Termeh, to finally leave Tehran. At one time, Reza had hopes that he and Termeh would have children to raise, but of late that dream was slipping away. Instead, they continued to live as two professionals pursuing different paths while sleeping in the same bed as husband and wife.

Reza's refuge was his dedication to his daily running workouts. He was looking forward to the hill repeat training that he and Heydar devised.

"I must say, this was a creative idea you had for us to do these hill repeats inside of the parking garage," commented Reza as the two runners jogged back down to the lower level.

"I thought that it would be a waste of time, all the driving to the edge of town where there are hills, when we have our own man-made hills right here in the city," said Heydar.

They reached the bottom and Heydar looked at his watch. "Four more seconds, are you ready?"

Before Reza could answer, Heydar's runner's watch beeped and they both set off to run up the spiral ramp to the fifth deck on their last of twelve repeat sprints to the top of the parking garage.

When they arrived at the top, both were nearly out of breath, but also satisfied they'd maintained relatively even intervals for each of the climbs. While jogging back down to the bottom followed by the one mile warm down stretch that took them back to the locker rooms of the university gym, they were finally able to have a normal conversation.

Reza enjoyed Heydar's company. Not just as a running partner, but also for being his sounding board and helping him work out some of the problems he faced with his work.

"Heydar?" Reza queried as they ran along at a relaxed pace, "Where did you get that new runner's watch with the feature that you set up for repeats with the countdown timer and the beep? I would like to have one also. I've had to change the battery on this old Casio two times already and I'm beginning to lose faith in it."

"It is nothing special. My sister sent it to me from the states. Here, take a look." Heydar unclipped the band and handed the watch over to Reza for inspection.

"I should be able to find one of these in Tehran next time I go there. Thank you, my friend," he said, handing the watch back to Heydar. "This project I've been working on has some speed bumps," he said to his friend.

"I thought your work at Natanz was finished, which is why you came here. This is not true?" Heydar asked.

"You must have misunderstood. We were still working out the

precise measures for machining the stainless steel tubing I told you about."

"The high-grade steel tubes for the bellows needed to make the gas?"

"Yes, those. We're close, though, and as you know, this is a critical piece for achieving the goal of peaceful, clean energy that will light up our cities at night."

"Reza, if I understand the situation correctly, you're also going to need some reliable computing to control and maintain the precision speeds required of the machines while they spin around together at very high speeds. Am I correct?"

"Exactly. We've been working on a monitoring system that could sense deviations within the closed network. I mean the slightest thing, such as a person turning on a bank of fluorescent lamps, is enough to cause changes in the current that supplies power to the machines spinning the materials. Everything has to be so tightly managed. This is a big problem for us."

"I'd offer some analysis and the entire pool of talent from the university if I thought your network wasn't closed. The eagerness of academic creativity seems so endless at times," Heydar said.

"That is the limitation I'm working with. We have our own team developing the command and control routines, but development is slow. This is the price of operating within a closed network. Perhaps together we can discover a way around these barriers," suggested Reza.

"Well, I'd have to know more about the architecture of the system in order to provide you with any useful advice," said Heydar.

Immediately after their workout routine, Reza was so pumped up, he allowed himself to raise sensitive topics with Heydar. He rationalized that it was only theoretical dialog.

"Heydar, maybe now that Termeh has moved to Isfahan and I don't have to commute to Tehran on Fridays, we could spend one of the weekend days on a long run together," Reza suggested.

"Yes, this is a wonderful idea. No more boredom from running fifteen miles alone. Instead, we can discuss our work on our runs, thus killing two birds with a single rock."

CHAPTER 8

Late Fall 2005 - Isfahan, Iran

Heydar had grown comfortable conversing with Reza about work during their long runs. He thought back to those earlier years and realized his role in their friendship was always to be the sounding board, and never the one to offer up challenges in his own work that he kept so close. His position at DP Iran allowed him to offer his expertise in ways that he believed would be beneficial to Reza.

When he was together with Reza discussing work, Heydar avoided sounding like he was eliciting information from his friend, but that was exactly his intent. He had to know how the command and control for the Natanz facility was managed. He was attempting to learn the possibilities for a point of entry to the Natanz facility computer network's management system.

When he graduated from NYU in the United States, Heydar

knew he should have been elated with the possibilities for the future that was before him, but he wasn't. He felt like a puppet. Heydar Pahlavi or "PeyLevy" wasn't born in Iran. His parents were from the small village of Ginosar, on the northern region of the Sea of Galilee. Heydar didn't like the fact that he wasn't in control of his destiny. He had very little say when Mossad Chief Meir Dagan personally authorized funds for Heydar to attend graduate school in France, where he studied computer science and disruption theory.

Immediately upon graduation, Heydar discovered that Mossad arranged a position for him to work for Siemens in Germany and then, with false identity and resume, was hired as a research assistant with DP Iran Co., landing him in Isfahan.

Due to his fortuitous relationship with Reza, Heydar quickly adapted to his responsibilities of keeping tabs on the developments of Iran's nuclear enrichment program. Specifically, as a source, he fed information back to Mossad through established contacts.

Heydar was leery of appearing overly interested in Reza's roll in Iran's uranium enrichment techniques. However, it suited him that Reza seemed to like that he knew enough about physics to ask the right questions when they were together.

"Those last three miles went by very fast, I hardly noticed," Reza said to Heydar as they continued the final miles of their workout.

"I enjoy listening to how you work out engineering problems. It helps me with my work as well," Heydar said.

Through self-study and conversation with Reza, Heydar had a genuine fascination with the process of uranium enrichment. It is in the understanding of uranium enrichment that Heydar built the illusion of a common passion.

"Heydar, I can't get over the simplicity of the concept and the complexity of the process. Basically, you dig uranium ore from the ground, which has similar appearance to iron. When it is enriched, it becomes a powerful energy source. Do you know how many doors will open for a nation dependent upon combustible energy sources?"

Heydar didn't have a chance to answer, instead, he watched and listened to Reza explain his version of nuclear enrichment. Heydar thought Reza would have made an excellent university professor. His dynamic style would certainly draw in the talents of the next generation of forward-thinking students.

Heydar was used to listening to Reza's flow of ideas while they ran. He played the part of the sounding board as Reza began to work through one of the concepts. "Come, let me show you what I mean." Reza stopped running and grabbed a stick. With it, he drew a flow chart in the soft dust.

"The first step of the process is to extract all the uranium from the ore, the end result being in the form of uranium oxide containing two isotopes of uranium, U-235 and U-238. It is the U-235 that is required for fueling a nuclear power plant," Reza explained while drawing an arrow pointing to a box he drew with the characters and letters for U-235.

When Reza stopped drawing, Heydar watched his friend raise an upturned hand as if he were holding an empty egg shell. "Mined uranium oxide is about ninety-nine percent U-238, so physicists and engineers like me have developed techniques to separate the small quantities of U-235 from the U-238. Once extracted, the U-235 must then be concentrated or enriched. As you know already, it is the sophisticated centrifuges that are the key mechanical component to the process," Reza told him.

Heydar had done some research of his own and learned that Farrouk Reza Khedem was one of Iran's top engineers in the specialized field of gas centrifuge engineering, so he never minded when Reza forgot that he'd already covered much of the enrichment process with him. He could feel Reza's enthusiasm coming through, and each time Reza explained something, Heydar learned just a bit more about the vulnerabilities and potential points of entry into the Natanz network.

He let Reza continue, "U-235 atomic weight shows that it weighs slightly less than U-238. By exploiting this weight difference, it is possible to separate the U-235 and the U-238. There are several steps in the process, including the use of hydrofluoric acid to create a gas form of uranium called uranium hexafluoride. It is the gas form of uranium that makes it possible to separate the isotopes in a centrifuge." Reza paused before going on.

"Since U-238 is slightly heavier than U-235, it is possible to separate the two by spinning them in a gas centrifuge at very high speeds. The uranium hexafluoride in the centrifuge has a slightly higher concentration of U-235, so it is removed and spun again in another centrifuge. This process is repeated several times in long cascades of centrifuges chained together." Heydar moved out of the way as Reza went at the dirt diagram again with the stick to illustrate the sequence of daisy chains.

Heydar looked up from the diagram to see Reza light up with a smile, "The advent of powerful precision computing has enabled the precise control needed to manage the spinning of the machine's equipment," said Reza, acknowledging that computing was Heydar's passion.

Aside from their shared interest in running, Heydar exploited the marriage of computer control and mechanical engineering that Reza kept coming back to and used it as the veneer needed to find that magical entryway into the command and control system at Natanz.

Heydar set off running again when Reza threw away the stick he was using to draw in the dirt. Then, Reza caught up to him, continuing his lecture. Even though it fell outside of his field of expertise, Reza explained the final steps of the enrichment process, which he believed to be much easier to achieve.

"Adding calcium to the hexafluoride gas results in two compounds, salt and enriched metalized uranium 235, which can be used as nuclear fuel for a reactor or a nuclear weapon," Reza explained.

It was this aspect of production that Heydar was most interested in. Not the process itself, but the amount of time before Iranian scientists would have a sufficient amount of enriched uranium to inform MISIRI, the Ministry of Intelligence and National Security of the Islamic Republic of Iran, so that their president Mahmoud Ahmadinejad could declare Iran a nuclear-powered nation.

CHAPTER 9

Late Fall 2005 - Data Processing Iran Co, Isfahan

Heydar reported back to his authorities each month. In return, he was provided with instructions through a different source each time. With the help of his counterparts in Israel, Heydar developed a system of conduits to funnel information in both directions between himself and the Mossad. His key agents were computer science students who were presumably vetted and recruited as interns by the academic development team at Data Processing Iran Co.

Throughout the academic year, groups of interns were accepted into the three-week program at DP Iran Co. Heydar received an introductory email from each of them at the beginning of their internship. When the students finished their three weeks and before their network accounts were closed with DP Iran Co, Heydar sent them each an email with a congratulatory message of thanks and good luck.

The elegance of the scheme worked beyond Heydar's expectations. The interns were provided with a discrete digital packet riding in the email as part of their signature block. The information packet was invisible to the network, but with a few lines of custom code, Heydar was able to extract the messages imbedded in the delivery packet, containing his instructions.

Most of the time the packets had a discrete binary code that translated to a null that Heydar knew meant that he was to proceed with his assignment as scheduled. However, on rare occasions, he received a different but equally discrete embedded code that instructed him to visit an online shopping website specializing in comic books. It was there, within the pages of adventure and fantasy comics, that Heydar received his explicit instructions.

Heydar also had a talent for imbedding code sequences of his own that would make their way back via the email sent to the interns at the end of their period of study. Anyone with a sense of curiosity might be able to examine the email and possibly find the embedded binary code, but it would be meaningless to them and hopefully assumed to be the product of junk that found its way into a stray server library that hadn't been cleaned out in years. To the uninitiated, stray code was like the plethora of RF energy that saturates the human environment. People send and receive email all the time and with an open system, it is common for junk code to ride along with it.

Haydar opened his daily email to awaken to a new challenge. His instructions were to reexamine alternative entries to a closed network where the server storage was analyzed and cleaned on a regular basis. For him, creating a backdoor into a closed system while lacking a mechanism such as hard wire, RF, WiFi, or any other kind of link to the outside and the Internet itself, required some creative thinking.

This would be a hurdle for Heydar, but not one that would prevent him from succeeding. What concerned him, though, was the timetable that his control authority put him on. He needed to deliver a plan back to them before the next intern was scheduled to graduate from the DP Iran Co. Program.

Heydar knew that his relationship with Reza was going to be crucial in the development of such a plan, one that would penetrate the closed computer network inside of the nuclear enrichment facility at Natanz.

CHAPTER 10

Spring 2005 - Arlington, Virginia

Major Mark Reynolds welcomed the early morning road trip from Langley Air Force Base to the Washington D.C. and the National Capitol Region. He thought of it as a break from the daily chaos of his duties as an action officer on the headquarters staff at Air Combat Command. His first six months flew by so fast, he was beginning to believe he'd be back at the controls of his Hog before acknowledging that he'd ever been flying a desk.

Mark wasn't the typical staff officer working out of a cubicle. Following his flash of brilliance fathering the FACE program during his first couple of weeks, his boss, Major General Glazer, wouldn't let him settle into advocating any of the boiler plated projects and programs usually ushered around by an enthusiastic "Iron Major." Mark found himself on a fast track with an early promotion to Lieutenant Colonel, so he was handed special projects on the fly. Most of them had difficult wrinkles to smooth out and nearly all of them were highly classified.

A DANGEROUS ELEMENT

Mark being a "pilot's pilot," wasn't terribly enthusiastic about the latest Unmanned Aerial Vehicle program Glazer wanted him to work on. He was already intimately familiar with the Predator program and what it took to convert it from a surveillance platform, to a laser designator, and finally to an all-in-one attack aircraft, armed with two ninety-pound Hellfire missiles.

He thought the Predator was the wrong aircraft for the Air Force to be investing so much. It was slow and only survivable in a purely permissive environment. In other words, in a combat environment where an enemy has the slightest ability to shoot back, Predators would be sitting ducks. Regardless, they seemed to be the readymade, reasonably priced solution that the ground commanders in Afghanistan kept asking for.

The program Glazer wanted Mark working on was the next generation of unmanned systems. Those working in the field of unmanned aviation considered Predators and Global Hawk UAV development to be analogous to the stage of development that manned powered aircraft were going through immediately following WWI.

The officers who were actually thinking about advancing air power were keen to get out of the rut that the Air Force found itself in with respect to UAVs.

The Air Force and Navy were still coming to grips with the advantages of using unmanned aircraft to do their dirty work. The thinking people in uniform put their minds against a better means of spying on activities in places where it wouldn't be politically acceptable to send in a manned aircraft. A pilot might get shot down and fall into the hands of a bad actor.

The Joint Unmanned Combat Aerial System, or JUCAS, was just such a system. It looked like a miniature version of the stealth B-2 bomber, only without a cockpit. Even though Mark wasn't a big fan of UAVs, he thought that if they were going to be of value in future conflicts, the Department of Defense was going to need them.

The industry partner engineers and the Air Force's Scientific Advisory Council frequently sought input from Lieutenant Colonel Reynolds because of his "out of the box" approach to evaluating operational problems. It was for this reason that he was directed to a high-rise in the Ballston neighborhood of Arlington, Virginia. While there, he was asked to consult with a team of scientists at the Defense Advanced Research Projects Agency.

When he arrived, Mark wasn't the least bit surprised to find his nemesis, Randy "Snake" Wormwood in attendance. He knew Snake claimed to be the originator of the arming of Predators with Hellfire missiles, but also knew that the story Snake told to the world about it was simply not true.

"Good morning, Coolhand, welcome to DARPA and this intimate little gathering. Coffee is on the counter at the back. You can make yourself at home and we'll get started in just a few," Snake said, standing at the door dressed in a grey suit and navy blue tie. Mark had to admit that the Snake had a knack for pouring on the charm, only he didn't buy it one bit.

Mark was still bitter about what happened that day in Afghanistan when Snake deviated from the mission and led his friend, Two-Tone, to his death. It took two years before the recovery of Tom Masterson's body enabled the Air Force to confirm his death and change his status from MIA to KIA. Even though Mark accepted the ultimate responsibility as flight lead, he held Snake in contempt for the loss of his friend.

"Good morning to you, too...Mr. Snake," Mark said to him as he maneuvered towards the counter where the coffee was waiting. He wasn't sure what the relationship was between Wormwood and DARPA, but suspected his role in the "other government agency" had something to do with covert operations. Some folks referred to Snake's organization as OGA, while others knew of it as an arm of the CIA. Regardless, Mark was pretty sure Snake acted in his own interest before considering the best interests of the United States.

Four other men and one woman all dressed in business attire entered the room after being greeted by Snake. Mark finished pouring himself a cup of coffee and took a seat at the oval conference table opposite a small screen.

All were seated when a frail and emaciated-looking older gentleman of about six feet and a couple of inches entered the room. The suits all stood to attention when Dr. Samuelson took his seat at the head of the table.

"Good morning, sir," said Snake as he maneuvered toward the front of the small conference room. "I suggest everyone introduce themselves before we get started with the scenario and begin brainstorming the possibilities, if that will be alright, sir."

"Please, proceed as you wish," Samuelson said.

As they went around the room, each of the five stated their name and professional affiliation. There was a scientist from Air Force Research Labs at Wright Patterson in Ohio and a representative from Navy Space and Naval Warfare Systems Command or SPAWAR in San Jose California. The two younger men both wore glasses and looked like they'd never seen the inside of a gym. They were Samuelson's protégés at DARPA and didn't offer much in the way of their specific fields of expertise. The attractively dressed and made-up woman who looked to be in her late thirties worked as a psychologist in the Defense Intelligence Agency's Human Intelligence Division. Mark didn't know what to make of her presence. He noticed that in spite of her appearance, she projected herself with an odd facial expression that gave the impression of disinterest.

Of course, there was Snake who took it upon himself to

facilitate the gathering. "Gentlemen, Lady, we're here to propose possibilities. There are no ideas too outlandish that can't be explored as we look at the hypothetical situation you'll see here in a moment."

Snake reached for a switch on a small podium and dimmed the lights in the small room. He picked up a remote and hit a button, transforming the screen at the foot of the oval table from black to a bright projection. It was a picture of the inside of a high-tech research facility. "What you see here is an image of an experimental research nuclear reactor," he said.

The facility was old and the equipment, which looked like it was used as a control station, looked antiquated. Mark and the others sitting around the table maintained their silence, anticipating what Snake was leading up to.

"You're probably thinking, 'So what? An old reactor from the 1960s.' But this particular one is located in Isfahan, Iran. We built it for the Iranians as part of a program called Atoms for Peace. Of course, that changed in 1979 and we all know the outcome."

Snake clicked the remote again. The next slide was a black and white photo that Mark recognized as an overhead image grabbed from a satellite in low-earth-orbit. The image had "Top Secret" stamped around the edges with some text information that included date, time, and geospatial data. There were no signs that the image had been analyzed or annotated by Intel specialists.

Mark realized that Snake's briefing began without any form of disclosure or security classification statements he'd grown used to hearing and seeing during this type of encounter. He figured it was an OGA thing to dispense with the boiler-plated security instructions. He also recognized it was consistent with Snake's style. He had to give Snake credit for respecting that those present would automatically know anything said in that room couldn't be leaked. It was a style that won the Snake an exclusive membership in the club of those who work and live behind the green door.

"Natanz, Iran," Snake announced, introducing the image in front of the small group. "This image was taken yesterday afternoon. These cranes you see here are specially designed to lower heavy equipment to depths in excess of two hundred feet below ground. He flashed to another overhead that looked similar to the previous image, only in place of the cranes, there were other types of digging equipment that Snake pointed out.

"Sources we've been working with have verified that the purpose of this facility is to enrich nuclear material. Not only are there developments above ground as you saw in both images, but the engineers working on Iran's nuclear program are preparing for underground testing, as you can see here in these images. If these facilities were being developed for peaceful energy production, there would be no need for an underground testing capability. Simply put, Iran is getting closer to producing a nuclear weapon and they intend to test it before using it to threaten the balance of regional power."

Snake sounded convincing. However, when Mark looked at the others sitting around the table, they appeared to be bored, as if they'd known all along what was going on in central Iran. Snake wasn't through with his picture show yet. He flipped back to the latest satellite image, drawing everyone's attention to a group of identical buildings.

"These buildings that you see here are specially designed to house daisy chains of centrifuges used to enrich nuclear material. How am I so sure of the purpose of these buildings, you ask?" In a flourish, Snake flashed up another slide advancing toward the end of his presentation. This image is a side by side of an enlarged section of the same area I just showed you, but this one is from Isère in the Occitan region of the French alps."

The buildings and structures in both images were remarkably identical. "They are getting closer and we are here to brainstorm ideas on how best to stop Iran's development of a nuclear weapon capability."

Then, Snake flashed another slide in front of the small group. It was a collage of photographs, each taken of different types of drones. "To get that deep into Iran, one option might be for us to use an unmanned aerial vehicle. How and what we would want it to do to disrupt the progress at these facilities are the questions we need to answer today."

Mark couldn't believe what he was hearing, especially given that he was surrounded by what he thought were some of the brightest and most imaginative minds gathered to examine the problem. Then, he looked around at the others in the room and realized that perhaps they were not at all creative or imaginative, but rather the only people who could be trusted with keeping a secret. The bottom line was, they needed to devise a plan for stopping the Iranians in their tracks.

The part Mark thought was ridiculous was Snake's immediate assumption that drones were the key to solving this operational problem. Regardless, he played along as the others in the room pitched their operational concepts. Mark thought one, in particular, had some merit. It came from one of the younger DARPA protégés.

"A stealth drone like the JUCAS penetrating at night could be a mother ship for one of these other vehicles," he said. "The small, stealth-flying wing has a range allowing it to get in and get out without detection. It could be launched from the deck of an Aegis Cruiser in the Persian Gulf and nobody would ever know."

"What about the parasite. The other vehicle?" Mark asked.

"That would be a different story. There are two possible approaches. Kinetic and non-kinetic disruptive. The first is easy. Use the VSTOL, vertical take-off and landing vehicle, to perch in a discrete location at the center of the facility. If it were packed with the right kind of explosives, it could be detonated several hours after being dropped from the mother ship. That way, any forensic analysis on the MISIRI would prevent the possibility of connecting the explosion with our stealth penetration, or tracing the event back to us," explained the young man.

Mark didn't like the first approach at all and could tell by the way it was pitched that it was part of an agenda Snake concocted. He looked at Dr. Samuelson for any sign of approval and noticed the older man remained stone-faced. Then, Mark asked the protégé about the second approach.

"The smaller vehicle would be equipped with an electromagnetic pulse capability. We locate a vulnerable and discrete location on one of the buildings used for housing a chain of centrifuges and send a pulse into the system, creating an anomaly in the spinning rate. We'd only need to do it one or two times. At the speeds the centrifuges spin, the abrupt changes in rotation velocity would be enough to destroy the complex in a cascading set of events," the young scientist stated.

"And the drone?" Mark asked.

"We program it to take off and fly out to an area where nobody will ever find it and have it self-destruct."

Mark looked at Snake for some sign that this might have been the first time he'd heard of this concept, but couldn't detect any change of expression, guessing that Snake had probably been a proponent of the approach. He then looked to Dr. Samuelson and asked, "Sir, you've heard of this proposal?"

Until now, the older man hadn't said a word since sitting at the table. He eyed Mark and said, "I've heard several variations of this general theme, yes. It seems to be one of the more viable options. We were asked to provide the National Command Authorities with options that do not include use of military force," he said.

Mark knew it meant that the President of the United States was the one interested in a solution. "Assuming the 'hypothetical scenario' that Mr. Wormwood introduced when we sat down could become an actual set of circumstances, how much time do we have?" Mark asked.

"I can answer that, sir," said Snake. "The Iranians harvested all of the spent fuel rods from the aging reactor at Isfahan. In fact, that reactor has been shut down now for about eight years. They've already been processing some of the nuclear material and spinning it. If they don't have any weapons-grade plutonium by now, they will by the end of the year."

"So, you're saying the clock is running and we need to take action within the year?"

"That is the status, yes," said Snake.

Mark turned to Dr. Samuelson and his two protégés, "I don't have an easy way to say this, sir, but I don't like either approach. If you'll allow me, I'm assuming that because we'd prefer a non-kinetic option, there are two goals: First, we need to prevent Iran from completing the enrichment of the materials, and second not get caught."

Samuelson turned to Mark and nodded. "Go on. You are correct."

Mark turned to the scientist from the Air Force Research Labs and spoke, "Whatever action we would take is only meant to disrupt their production. Disrupt." He said the word with some finality in a low tone, as if he were still thinking about something related, when the light bulb came on for him.

For the first time, the bored-looking psychologist woman looked up from her hands folded in her lap. She gave Reynolds her full attention.

With a spark of renewed energy, Mark looked to everyone in the room in turn, including Snake. "We want to be able to come back and do this again, to 'disrupt' Iran's development. Let them get almost to the end before causing the facility to experience a malfunction that would ruin everything." He paused to let the idea sink in.

"Their scientists and engineering analysts can scratch their heads for a while before returning to the drawing board. Later, maybe five years out, we do it again. We'll make them think they've made some mistakes with their engineering of the centrifuge bearings or the speed management control software their computers use to keep the centrifuges spinning at a balanced rate. That is it," he said. "Our logical point of entry is the host network controlling the machines at the facility."

The room was quiet for a long moment before Wormwood cracked a smirk and said to his former colleague and squadron mate, "Well, you seem to have discovered the crux of the issue, old buddy. Our sources have verified that the network at that facility is closed up tight, just as we'd anticipated. There is no way of getting at it, which is why we've been investigating the concentrated magnetic pulse option."

The room went silent again. The female psychologist kept looking at Mark, waiting to hear what he was going to say next – and she wasn't disappointed.

"Going that deep into Iran with a drone is like sending a bull into the china store. We're going to get caught if we take that approach, you can almost be sure of it," declared Mark.

Dr. Samuelson turned to Mark and said, "Colonel, we're here to discuss possible solutions. Not throw darts at the proposals on the table."

Mark knew the older gentleman was right and apologized immediately, "Sir, what I meant was there has to be a better way. The technologies that are available right at this moment are even being exploited by the commercial market. I want to believe we could come up with something more discrete. Scratch that. I know we can. I'm suggesting that if UPS and FedEx can use RFID to remotely scan and track packages, there's got to be a way to leverage something like that to get inside a computer network."

"And when you penetrate that network, then what? Do what with it?" Wormwood shot back. Mark knew that Snake was dead set on using his drone concept to carry out the mission.

"Just thinking out loud...wouldn't it be cool if a small piece of code could be inserted into the control software? Something with a perturbation function imbedded in it. Nothing big, just a small phugoid that would, at some point, become large enough to create an imbalance in the mechanical systems."

"As if they would notice a small drone hidden on a rooftop and not see this 'phugoid' you mention destroying their precious facility while they watch." Snake wagged his head from side to side while looking at the ceiling. "The monitoring capability at that enrichment facility is bound to have alarms and failsafe systems that would uncover your proposed tactic long before any damage could be done," Snake postulated.

Before Mark could say more, one of Samuelson's protégés leaned over the table and said, "This is brilliant."

The scientist from AFRL chimed in as well, "We could develop a mask that prevents the monitors from seeing any changes in the spinning rates."

"Exactly, a record and play loop like the kind we've all seen in heist movies where the thieves insert a looping video into the camera surveillance system so that the security folks wouldn't see what was actually happening. They remain in the dark, believing all is well," said the other protégé.

"It could work," said the Air Force scientist. "We'd need to know a bit more about the control system's software and do some testing, but with the teams we have conducting similar sorts of modeling and simulation at MIT, I think it could be done fairly easily."

"That would leave just one thing remaining," Mark said.

"Delivery," replied Dr. Samuelson. "The long pole that got this conversation started in the first place."

Snake looked at his watch and said, "Gentlemen, Lady, the Doctor and I have another engagement to attend. We thank you for your interest and you can look forward to joining us again in a few weeks." He crossed his arms and looked directly at his old squadron mate, Coolhand, and nodded to indicate that it was time for everyone to leave. Dr. Samuelson stood and shook hands with Mark, the AFRL representative and the psychologist from the DIA as they departed. Snake remained behind with the two smart guys from DARPA.

Mark and the others left the building at the same time. They had to turn in their security badges and retrieve their cell phones and personal items from the entry control where they left them before the meeting.

"Colonel Reynolds?" It was the voice of the female psychologist. He paused in his tracks and turned to see what she wanted.

"I'm sorry, we really didn't get to properly meet each other earlier," said Rachel Jennings.

Mark stood on the sidewalk out front of the high-rise waiting for her to catch up. He noticed that she wasn't a strikingly beautiful woman, but she did appear to be athletic and looked attractive enough in her tailored grey skirt and blazer combo.

"Ms. Jennings, did you need a ride or something?" he asked. "I drove and I'm not expected back at Langley anytime soon," he offered.

"No, thank you. I have a car. I'm not going back across the river right away either. I just needed to ask you something," she said, noticing Mark looking around, making sure they wouldn't be overheard. She gave him a slight grin and suppressing a giggle, "It isn't anything about the meeting. No, I was just curious how you got invited."

"I wasn't. I was directed to come up here." He shouldn't have been surprised at her question. Already the morning had started out a bit strange.

"Oh, I should have known. Well, it seemed you and Mr.

Wormwood have some history and I thought…"

"Just coincidence. Guys like Wormwood always seem to show up when there's a chance for some action. He's a glory hound, you know."

"Yes, I noticed."

"So, Ms. Jennings, my turn. How did you get invited, or were you directed also?"

"Same as you. I've been to a few of these in the past and my boss likes my reports, so he keeps sending me to represent his interests. He and that gentlemen you met, the one that sat at the head of the table, don't exactly see eye to eye."

Mark turned and started walking toward the side street where he parked his car. Ms. Jennings kept pace with him, even though she'd parked on a street in the opposite direction.

"Was there something else you wanted to ask?" Mark offered.

"Well, yes, I mean, no. Let me start over. Don't take this the wrong way, but for a guy who flies jets, you seem to have quite a bit of experience working out technical problems. Like I said, I've been to a lot of these engagements lately and in my experience, most of the operators, regardless of the service they belong to, tend not to be very creative," she said.

Rachel continued, "There is a series of War Games, Virtual War Games my boss is sponsoring at Fort Belvoir next month. I was wondering if you might be interested in participating. I could get you an invite if you are," she said with a doe-eyed look that would be hard to turn down.

"Ms. Jennings…"

"Rachel. Please, call me Rachel," she interrupted.

"Okay, Rachel, I don't really have the luxury of deciding how I spend my working hours. You'll have to go through the A-8 at Langley and someone higher up the food chain than you or I in order to request me by name. Otherwise, I'd say yes to your invitation," he said.

"Great. Don't plan any leave for the next month. I'm sure you'll enjoy the experience." She reached out to shake hands with Mark before he unlocked the door to his car. Then, she turned and strode off in the opposite direction.

Strange woman, Mark thought. He didn't expect to see her again, as he didn't believe someone that young and with her background would have the pull to get Major General Glazer to release him to play in some other agency's reindeer games. He was pretty sure he was sent on this little errand today only because drones were on the agenda, and he knew Glazer hated the robot aircraft almost as much as he did.

CHAPTER 11

Spring 2005 - Arlington, Virginia - DARPA

After Dr. Sameulson, Mark Reynolds and the others left the room, Snake turned to the two others who remained behind and said, "Shut the door. I'm going to make this brief. I'm running the only agent who is in contact with our source in Iran. We need to know from our partners if human delivery is possible. I'm going to need a team at the ready to develop a tech solution as soon as we can verify a few things. I'll see you both in my office later this afternoon."

The DARPA boys left the room. Snake pulled the flash stick from the drive on the projector and sat down in the chair at the head of the table where Dr. Samuelson was seated earlier. Even though he was dead set on using drones to penetrate the denied area in Iran, he realized that the solution they'd come up with was the best one. True to form, he wanted to be the one to lead the operation, even though he realized he was no longer in possession of the expertise needed to carry out the mission.

A short while later, Snake showed up at his boss, Hardesty's office, to debrief what came out of the brainstorming session.

Snake's relationship to his boss went back to the days when he was still on active duty flying F-16s. He reflected back to those days when Hardesty brought him under his wing. Snake knew his days in the Air Force were waning and jumped on Hardesty's offer to come to work at the CIA. He didn't disappoint his boss either, quickly proving himself when he recruited an agent that consistently provided him with access to reliable sources in the Middle East. Though Hardesty had no idea who some of Snake's trusted agents were, he'd grown used to the rookie's ability to deliver. The agent Snake had been running set him up for success with Hardesty. The man called himself Marios.

In his early days with the CIA, Snake was the beneficiary of Hardesty's past. When Beirut started to come apart in '82, Hardesty was there to pick up the pieces. The many agents he ran out of Beirut scattered to the winds. The first mission Hardesty sent Snake on was to Larnaca, Cyprus. His orders were to scarf up what was left of a network of former Cold War agents and find a way to keep them on the payroll.

With Snake's version of loyalty that most professionals develop over time, he stood by to accept the orders his boss, Hardesty, gave him.

"See if our source thinks it might be possible to sneak something into the facility. Something small, like a designer pen or wristwatch, something of that nature. We've got to get a device close enough to a piece of computer equipment that is linked to that network. It could even be as simple as interfacing with a printer's buffer system. Assuming the printer or whatever device we target is online, we may just get lucky enough to find a way in.

CHAPTER 12

Winter 2006 - Fort Belvoir, Virginia

He read the first line of the memo again. It was addressed to him, Lieutenant Colonel Mark Reynolds. Reading his own title made him feel old, even though he wasn't.

Unfortunately for Mark, the fast track that the brass at Air Combat Command put him on kept him away from the cockpit. Mercifully, it also prevented him from having to trudge along as a staff officer. He reflected back on the year and a half it had been since he was called into Glazer's office following his first brainstorming session with DARPA. At the time, he thought he was being summoned so that he could be told he'd be participating in a series of war-gaming exercises, but instead it was something completely different.

Coolhand listened patiently as Major General Glazer told him why he was being sent to RAND as a Department of Defense

Liaison in lieu of attending Air War College.

"You're out of cycle to attend War College at Maxwell and you probably wouldn't like it anyway. Doing some research with RAND is a better fit for you. I wish we could keep you around, but orders are orders. You do know what this means don't you?" the general asked him.

"Sir, it means at least one more year out of the cockpit if that is what you're referring to."

"You really are the genuine deal," Glazer said. "I thought all you fast burners knew that War College or the equivalent in residence meant you were going to be a sure bet for full bird. Anyway, good luck." Glazer shook his hand and sent him on his way.

To Mark, it seemed like yesterday that it all went down. The job at RAND and then a couple of weeks of leave spinning his wheels before capping off all the academics with a trip to the Joint Forces Staff College. He still couldn't figure out why he was sent there. He hadn't had a joint staff job and wasn't a planner. His guess was the Air Force didn't really know what to do with him, so they entered him into another term of Professional Military Education to buy time while looking for a suitable assignment for him to fill.

The Joint Forces Staff College came and went and Mark was again spinning wheels between assignments. Without a family to plan logistics around and the fact that it was winter time, Mark didn't want to waste leave. He knew trying to hook up with Anne and Charles in order to see his daughters would be futile. He figured they'd be too pre-occupied with school to spend time with him, so he didn't even try to visit them in Colorado.

Instead, he pondered the irony of having finally been tracked down by Rachel Jennings. He allowed her to recruit him as a participant at Fort Belvoir's brand new joint war gaming center. The first time he heard the term "virtual sand table," he had visions of a large room with a glass touch screen table. He imagined it would look identical to the gaming tables of old where there was actual sand and miniature pieces of military hardware for the gamers to stage in various positions.

It was his third visit, and he found himself getting comfortable with the workstations set up in an amphitheater with projection screens everywhere. Each participant was required to war game a list of scenarios using various combinations of developmental capability over the course of a week's time.

Following each of the sessions, Mark thought it was interesting that none of the participants were given any feedback. There were no outcomes or debriefing of results. He'd become bored with the entire process and was looking forward to receiving an assignment soon.

It didn't help that Randy "Snake" Wormwood kept showing

up at the games. Even though Snake wasn't present for every session, he was around enough for Coolhand to get a strong case of the creeps. He felt he had to look over his shoulder in case Snake was about to pull something.

One item on the gaming list drew Mark's attention. It was a capability in the human intelligence category. The one item seemed to be on the previous list in a different category. He thought maybe there was a designer pharmaceutical research and manufacturer that was paying some lobbyists. He knew he wasn't the only officer who noticed how some District Congressmen sitting on the House Armed Services Committee managed to earmark additional funding to keep certain companies afloat.

Prior to each session, the small group of war-gaming participants was "read in" to the various compartments of the top-secret capabilities they'd be evaluating. The list of classified words that Mark could never say aloud was growing. For instance, he was reminded that the program called MV-ULTRA didn't exist. He always laughed to himself when he heard the security briefers say a program didn't exist, particularly when they'd continue with a detailed description of the non-existent capability.

The other curiosity that drew his attention was Rachel Jennings. He recognized her even with her new, close-cropped hairstyle. She entered the room just after the security briefing and sat just a few feet away from Mark. He wasn't sure why she didn't acknowledge him. He thought certainly if she were involved in the gaming exercises, she'd have seen his name on the roster of participants.

A briefer entered the room and flashed a few slides up on the screen explaining the origins of the MV-ULTRA capability. It was a derivative of a program called MK-ULTRA that originated in the 1950's. The briefer went on describing some of the goals and effects of the program.

"The initiatives under the MK-ULTRA program included the development of substances intended for ingestion by human beings in order to control thought and behavior. In those years, the scientists and subjects referred to the experiments as mind control. How many of you have heard rumors of this type of program?" asked the briefer.

Only a couple of hands went up from participants wearing business attire. Nobody wearing a uniform wanted to believe that their government would use such tactics.

The briefer continued, "MK-ULTRA had its place in the Cold War, and it enabled access to sources and information that may have prevented nuclear exchange during the Cuban Missile Crisis. In those times, one of the outcomes sought after by the human intelligence operatives was the combination of effects. Specifically, those exhibited by the target when their inhibitions were lowered. All test subject's symptoms were consistently followed by an amnesia effect when the drug wore off. Of course, there were other versions tailored for use by operatives with specific needs," the briefer paused, hoping for some questions before going on. He wasn't disappointed.

"I've heard rumor that versions of this program are still underway. Is this true?" asked one of the participants who was dressed in business attire.

The briefer had a canned answer, knowing this question would come up. "MK-ULTRA was officially terminated in 1973. The CIA was coming under fire at the time for a variety of other questionable practices. The entire country was dealing with the hallucinogenic drug epidemic, and many of our soldiers both in and returning from Vietnam had become addicted to hard drugs."

"You didn't answer the question," Mark fired back. "This capability is on the list for the war games along with the others."

"Sir, I'm just the briefer," said the young intelligence analyst, eager to complete his briefing.

"Just one more question that we'll need some clarification on if we're to provide an honest assessment of these capabilities," a Navy Commander put forward. "What would be the delivery methods and options if MV-ULTRA were available in our bag of tricks?"

"We were just getting to that." The briefer flashed up another chart with a list of 'tailored' capabilities that could be included under MV-ULTRA when used against an adversary. Some of these were designed to diminish or negate the effects of alcohol on the user. Others included outcomes similar to the 'date rape' drug that hit the media in recent years.

The briefer continued, "For example, one way to administer this weapon against a target is tactile delivery. For lack of a better word, we'll refer to the substance as a drug, which is an oily film, virtually invisible, tasteless and without aroma.

We've learned through experimentation on lab animals that tactile contact can be very effective. The drug can be smeared on an object that the target might come in contact with. The oily base dries immediately and liquefies almost imperceptibly when in contact with living tissue. The key is that this drug can be rapidly absorbed through the skin resulting in an immediate effect."

The young intelligence briefer then switched through several more slides illustrating possible scenarios for delivery and use of the MV-ULTRA capability. "I'm partial to the method of learning the target's behavior to the point of finding out what objects in their possession they tend to handle on a predictable basis."

The image on the screen showed a woman in a business suit standing on a busy urban sidewalk, talking on a cell phone. "Two issues when administering the drug with a device such as a cell phone. First, for the operative to get access to it without raising suspicion could be problematic. Second, it is much more difficult to predict when the target would come in contact with the device."

The next image was of a man opening a car door. "As you can see, his bare fingers lifting the lever suggest sufficient contact and pressure for complete absorption. Risk is low for the operative since the weapon can easily be deployed when the target isn't present."

"What about collateral damage?" asked an Army Officer.

"You mean someone besides the intended target coming into contact with the weapon?" the intelligence officer asked without waiting for a response. "That is a risk just as is any other activity during a HUMINT operation. We've studied this issue and that is part of the war gaming we'll be doing this week. We'll examine probabilities and consequences associated with the various delivery options. The goal is to come up with a list of viable options for our operatives, should we determine this weapon has merit."

Changing the pace of the briefing, the young officer switched back to the list of capabilities and proceeded to cover each of them in turn. A couple of them were humorous, such as the "Love Cloud" delivered by means similar to tear gas designed to overcome civil disturbances. It was a gas that produced a euphoric effect on the adversary.

Another was based on the same concept, but had no practical application. Poison the water supply with a substance that makes everyone gay, so they wouldn't want to hurt one another. There wasn't a person who didn't laugh out loud when they came to that one on the list. "What does being gay have to do with hurting or not hurting people?" shouted a Navy officer from the back of the room.

There was another weapon listed for use during civil disturbances and riot control. It was an expanding foamy substance delivered via fire hoses that was designed to create confusion and disorientation. A watery substance would be shot from a nozzle, and upon contact with an oxygenated environment, it would expand into harmless bubbly foam creating a layer four to five feet deep. This capability didn't make any of the war gamers laugh, but all of them commented that it would be difficult to clean up, thus having limited application.

Mark noticed Rachel Jennings remained in attendance during all of the sessions. She finally got around to acknowledging that she remembered him just prior to the lunch break on the first day.

"Well, I made it. Better late than never," Coolhand said to her while they all headed out of the building to get some fresh air.

"How've you been, Colonel?"

"Busy and not so busy, I guess. Sometimes it seems like we spin our wheels," he replied.

"You wouldn't say that if you were in my shoes."

He noticed that in spite of her well-dressed and made-up appearance, she had lines on her face and tired eyes, more so than the first time they met in Arlington. "I take it you're working too hard. Not enough sleep. Not enough time off. When was the last time you took a vacation?"

"Oh, gosh. It's been awhile. Coffee? A bite to eat? I missed breakfast and I'm feeling famished. Low blood sugar is warning me to grab a bite," she said.

"Alright, you lead the way. I could use some brain food," he said as she led him to another building where there was a small cafeteria.

Over lunch they made small talk and caught up on what each of them had been doing during the eighteen months since they discussed the Iranian centrifuge problem. Mark wasn't surprised to notice Rachel didn't have a wedding ring. Changing the subject, he asked, "Why isn't an attractive professional like you married?"

She looked away from him for a brief moment, cracking a small smile of embarrassment. "I was," she said. "Married, that is, if you could call two months and an annulment a marriage."

"Sorry, I shouldn't have pried."

"It's alright. It was a long time ago. I was young and foolish. Fresh out of school with a decent paycheck. Ed wasn't a bad guy. He just had no ambition. I came home one day to the smell of marijuana wafting through the air, and Ed was on the couch in a funk with cartoons blaring from the television. I knew I couldn't have this going on under our roof. Such habits would have been bad for my career and I couldn't see Ed turning himself around anytime soon. You can probably tell I'm not the nurturing type," she needed to vent.

"Well, you should be thinking about rewarding yourself with a vacation sometime soon. Someplace sunny, maybe," he said, attempting to lighten the mood.

"Do you see your wife and daughters often?" she asked.

"Ah, I should ask you how you knew about my family since we've never talked about it, but then I should have known you probably know everything about each participant on this week's roster. Anyway, I don't see them as much as I'd like. Anne got remarried shortly after the divorce. Charles, her husband, is a really good man and treats the girls well. I try not to interfere. The girls are at that age where they prefer spending more time with friends than with family."

"So, we're quite a pair aren't we?" commented Rachel.

"Free and easy. Takes the trouble out of all the moving around. I've got a car, a laptop, a place to sleep and a tennis racket. It's all I really need since the Air Force has kept me moving around, studying and doing research. I don't even know if I would remember how to fly a plane anymore it's been so long."

"Well, it's a good thing you're available."

"And why might that be?" he asked. "Do you know something I should know?"

"You'll find out soon enough, I only know that I heard your name at the Defence Intelligence Agency. Who knows, we may end up working for the same people."

"I thought we already did," said Mark with a hint of sarcasm. He wasn't a big fan of the DIA and liked reminding people that by working in the same department, service members and civil servants alike, everyone needs to be on the same side trying to do what is best for the country.

"Well, we'd better get back," she said. "The sand tables await."

"Rachel?"

She looked up at him, waiting.

"What are you doing here anyway?" he asked.

"Colonel Reynolds, it is really complicated. You know where I work. The DIA is in the business of collecting information about other countries and their people, the influential ones. There are lots of spies in our midst," she said.

"Yes, but that doesn't explain the need for a psychologist. The psychologists we had at Air Combat Command were part of the support forces at field hospitals. There weren't any on the headquarters staff. So, you have a duty description and I'm curious about just what that might be."

"It's in another one of those classified compartments with a Top Secret letter designation." It was clear she couldn't elaborate and didn't want to, even if she could.

Mark figured whatever the details were that related to her work probably had something to do with her quirky appearance. She wore a look of someone in need of a good night's sleep. The two of them returned to the gaming facility without further conversation.

CHAPTER 13

Spring 2006 - Isfahan, Iran

Heydar PeyLevy just finished composing an email praising the intern who just graduated from the latest curriculum he had created for those he worked for at DP Iran Co. His superiors were pleased with the results of his training program. On the other end of Heydar's secret second life was the latest coded message he received from Tel Aviv.

The request was the first big risk Heydar faced since building his long relationship with Reza. The connection gave Mossad access to untold volumes of information that he'd gleaned from his nuclear engineer friend.

Now, Heydar was being asked to use Reza to penetrate the tightly closed computer network at Natanz. Until now, there was no danger to Heydar or Reza. However, to get inside a closed network meant he would have to develop a means of physical entry. Reza was the key.

It took an additional two months communicating back and forth with Tel Aviv to develop an operations plan. He used his method of correspondence with the interns to confirm the plan. Though cryptic, the last message he received put him on a timetable that required a visit with a team of computer scientists and a small group of nano-technologists.

It had been years since Heydar had any occasion to leave Iran. His last trip outside of Iran was over eight years ago, before he ever met Reza. While fresh from the European University, Heydar still had contacts with a group of software developers. He'd gone to Baku, Azerbaijan to meet with one of the talented developers who specialized in Peripheral Interface Controlling. Heydar had been studying the elegance of Reduced Instruction Set Computing. The matching interests in PIC and RISC were a natural fit.

While in Baku, Heydar was recruited by Mossad. The story behind the recruitment and the manipulation that went along with it boiled down to one thing - money. When he was an undergraduate, his father was a civil servant in the ministry of settlement and agriculture. Though not rich, the PeyLevy family was able to support Heydar's education and the care for his younger sister who developed a mild case of schizophrenia six months prior to her nineteenth birthday.

When Heydar's father suddenly died of a heart attack, it was only a couple of weeks later that his mother committed suicide by jumping from the family's sixth floor balcony.

Those interested in Heydar's scientific talents now had the lever they needed to get him to work for them. They told him his sister would be provided with the best of care for the remainder of her life if he agreed without question, to the work assignments he was given. He saw no harm in what he was doing since none of the projects impacted the people he was working with personally.

One of the side benefits of his friendship with Reza was that Heydar managed to stay in top physical condition. The two of them agreed several years ago that they would run the New York City Marathon together in 2010. It was a dream that they both kept alive. It served as a purpose for the long runs they ran every other Saturday.

"Summer is going to be here before long," said Reza with a steady breath as he paced smoothly through the first few meters of a twenty-five kilometer run the two men set out on.

"It means we'll have to start planting water caches in order to keep to our training plan," Heydar added.

"How is your work at DP these days?" Reza asked. "Will you have interns to help with the new training curriculum this summer?" Reza wanted to show interest in the things his closest friend spent the bulk of his time doing.

"Work is work. It's a grind. Sometimes it seems like we do the same things over and over again. Occasionally, there are small adjustments needed to keep things interesting, but if it weren't for the interns, I would not enjoy this kind of work. Everyone needs a job, though, and we've got New York to look forward to."

"Yes, New York," said Reza in deep thought. He was imagining the distance. "Twice as far away as France."

Reza didn't notice that Heydar picked up the pace a little. After the turn around and heading back to the university stadium, Heydar became more talkative.

"When the academic season is finished next month, I'm going to take a vacation," declared Heydar.

It had never occurred to Reza that his running partner had a private life outside of work and their mutual love for running. Reza thought back and realized he'd never said much to his friend about the vacations he'd endured with Termeh. Most men loved to be away from work, but Reza wasn't the type that could relax if he were away from work very long. The project at Natanz was his baby.

"Where will you go?" Reza asked about Heydar's vacation plans.

"I've been thinking about this for some time. One of the interns was from Larnaca, Cyprus. His family has a villa on a rocky hill overlooking the Mediterranean Sea. He showed me a picture. I received an invitation from his parents to attend his graduation reception and they offered to have me stay as a guest."

"That sounds fantastic," Reza added, "I've never seen Cyprus, and it has been a very long time since I've been on a beach other than the rocky shores of the Caspian."

The two men were nearing the end of their long run and slowed to a walk for the last couple hundred meters.

"You'll of course keep up with the training while you're on holiday," Reza stated.

"Yes, yes, of course. I'll take pictures and we'll be ready to run together throughout the long, hot summer as we always do."

For the next few weeks, Heydar's Cyprus vacation was one of the topics they gravitated toward when conversing together on their longer runs. The other topic was Reza's mounting concern over the work he'd been involved in at Natanz.

"When we talk about your work, you seem troubled. I always think of you as the man who has everything under control," Heydar said to him.

"The enrichment of the uranium is going well, yes. The development of peaceful uses for the magic coming from the nuclear fuel has been a dream of mine since I was a boy. I cannot put my finger on it, Heydar, but the mood at the facility has been changing right under my nose. I must have been blind. There have been visits by high-ranking officials from The Atomic Energy Organization of Iran, as well as the Ministry of Defense."

"How is that different from before? You've always had visitors to deal with. I remember just this past winter how you were nervous about jumping through so many hoops to prepare a presentation about the centrifuge controls," said Heydar, reminding his friend of past events while eliciting new information about the attention the Iranian government officials were paying to the project at Natanz.

"There is a man I knew from Tehran who's been coming more often lately," Reza said in a contemplative tone. "I met this man at a dinner party that Termeh was invited to several years ago. During her graduate studies, the department chair from the Shahid Beheshti University of Medical Sciences and Health Services opened her home to Termeh and the other students who would soon graduate. It just so happens that this professor was married to the man who is now coming to Natanz. I looked up Termeh's professor's name and there he was, Dr. Hadazi's husband, Arman Hadazi, head of ballistic missile development for Shahid Bagheri Industrial Group."

"So, you're worried that the work you are doing is drawing the interest of those who are no longer interested in peaceful uses for this technology?" asked Heydar.

"Perhaps. I don't know what I think anymore. It is as if I had been sleeping and suddenly woke up to notice the increases in security and the questions that come from the visitors. I'm glad I don't have to go out to Natanz more than I do. It is so uncomfortable there. The officials from AEOI asked if the bearing configurations we designed for the centrifuges could withstand an increase in speed."

Reza's director had all the chief scientists and engineers relocate their offices to Isfahan so that they could continue interaction with the latest developments in technology at the university. He didn't know that the move was intended to keep as few eyes as possible on the progress of work taking place out at the facility.

"We've all been put on a new production schedule so that the new fuel can be made available perhaps as early as a year from now."

When Reza made his weekly trips, he confined his visits to the banks of centrifuges and the adjoining control facilities. He took little notice of the digging that had been going on near the western end of the facility.

Heydar could see the strain in Reza's eyes and the increasing depth in the lines on his face. "Your concern seems to involve more than having to work harder and longer hours," said Heydar, fishing for more.

Reza took the bait. "It is dangerous. Too dangerous to risk all that we've worked for. The processors in the system control aren't fast enough to keep up. An out of phase oscillation of any kind at those speeds would be enough to destroy everything, but that isn't the biggest problem. If the U-235 gas leaks out of the containment of the rotor tubing while spinning at such high speed, the entire complex could become contaminated with nuclear radiation and turn Natanz into another Chernobyl."

***

Two months later, when Heydar met his contact at Larnaca International Airport in Cyprus, he was not surprised that this person was of unknown origin and held citizenship as a Cypriot. He knew he wouldn't be visiting with the intern whose family presumably invited him to visit. The entire affair was arranged to foil the Iranian agents he assumed would be assigned to monitor his movements. Not that he raised suspicion within Iranian channels, but Heydar knew that all professionals in the technical professions were monitored whenever they had occasion to leave Iran.

It was a simple task for the small Iranian surveillance contingent based in Cyprus to confirm that Heydar Pahlavi's visit was legitimate. He couldn't be a hundred percent sure, but he thought he spotted a surveillance team. He avoided looking in their direction and assumed his presence wasn't even a blip on the radar for the man and woman duo.

Heydar's contact drove him to the villa just off the highway in the southern foothills of the Troodos. There, they spent the better part of two days lounging beside a swimming pool on a patio overlooking the Mediterranean in the distance. Even though Heydar laid out his concerns about the recent increases in security at the Natanz facility that he'd learned of from Reza, the Cypriot, or more accurately, the mysterious agent, was more interested in Reza's lifestyle.

Heydar told him what he knew. The agent who called himself Marios was looking for hooks or chinks in Reza's professional armor. He needed something that could be exploited without raising suspicion. He asked Heydar what he knew of Reza's marriage and if there were any indiscretions.

"I've known this man for over five years," Heydar said. "I wouldn't say he's had a rocky marriage. To be honest, his marital relationship is probably no different than other arranged marriages in the traditions of Islamic Families."

"No children, then?"

"None."

"Look, to get access to a command and control system inside of a closed network, we need physical access. Now, I can tell you that with the resources you have access to, you should be able to find some clever people who can do something like what I'm about to suggest."

"I'm listening," said Marios.

"Farrokh Reza Khadem is a loyal professional. Not necessarily loyal to his government, but loyal to his cause, which is clean energy for Iran. We're not going to be able to manipulate him to do anything for us that he believes could be dishonest. If we're going to use him, it has to be without his knowledge."

"Go on, continue," said Marios.

"Reza is a runner. He's also technically-minded and likes small, elegant things that perform simple tasks. When I first met him, he wore a black Casio digital chronometer during our runs. He kept track of every split for every kilometer that we ran together. He always did some post-workout analysis in his head, because our training sessions often had the feel of having been engineered to achieve specific objectives, especially when we did repeat intervals on the track at the university."

"I don't see where you're going with this," said Marios.

"Hear me out. You cannot easily purchase a sophisticated runner's watch in Isfahan Iran, and Reza wouldn't even know where to start looking in Tehran. My proposal calls for some sort of emission capability using nano-technology. Maybe it could be imbedded in a runner's watch that has all the features that a runner like Reza would appreciate."

When Heydar paused, waiting for a response from Marios, he could see that the man was thinking. Marios thought it was remarkable that a guy like Heydar, so far away and disconnected from the think tanks in Washington D.C., could come up with a solution that started to sound remarkably like the one his handler, Randy Wormwood, asked him to look into a couple of months ago.

Heydar watched Marios who appeared to be in deep thought before he finally spoke, "I like this idea of yours. I wonder, don't the staff members and employees at places like Natanz have to remove all personal items and dress in protective clothing before entering pure, clean spaces required for their kind of work?"

"Yes, normally that is true. However, Reza is now a fairly senior engineer. In fact, he's in charge of facility operations. He spends most of his time at an office in Isfahan near the old reactor facility. He goes to Natanz about once or twice each week and spends most of his time in an office there, rarely entering the sanitized areas of the facility."

"How do you know this?" asked the Cypriot.

"I've pieced things together over a long period of interactions with Reza. He's become more and more frustrated lately and says things that give me a broader view of his working life. I think he's just happy to have someone he can open up to."

"This office he has at Natanz..." Marios was pondering. "Is the computer he uses there connected to the closed network we're needing to get into, do you think?"

"I'm certain that it is. Based on everything he's told me, the firewalls are set up so that once inside the facility itself, the engineers have seamless access so that they can easily retrieve data needed for the modifications they've been asked to perfect to speed up the centrifuges."

"Okay, I think we are finished here, for now," said Marios. "Enjoy the sun and the rest of your stay on Cyprus."

When Heydar returned to Larnaca International Airport for his return to Tehran, his already olive-toned skin was a shade darker. Wearing sunglasses, blue jeans and an oversized white, cotton dress shirt with buttons open at the top, he looked like a man who'd enjoyed a Cypriot holiday.

He knew his act must have been working for him when he noticed the same middle-aged Iranian couple sitting across from one another at a bistro table. It was all the confirmation he needed to know they'd been assigned to maintain surveillance of Iranians traveling through Cyprus. He watched them as he walked past and they barely gave him notice. He figured they would later report and submit a request to have someone confirm his arrival back at Tehran and his return to work at DP Iran Co in Isfahan.

***

LAMB

TOP SECRET/SCI: HUMINT RPT
DTG 0709015z0506
Classification// TS/SCI: HUMINT RPT/ Eyes Only

//FM: Marios//

//TO: R. Wormwood/Deputy Director/Mid-East Field Desk//

//SUBJ: Iranian Contact//

A. Point of Entry

1. Source indicated possible point of entry. Operative inside of Natanz facility is easily distracted by his past time activies.

2. Inform DARPA engineering team - recommend using a common plastic running watch for required device platform.

//END OF MSG//

TOP SECRET/SCI: HUMINT RPT
Handle VIA EYES ONLY - DESTROY IMMEDIATLY AFTER READING

CHAPTER 14

Summer 2008 - Arlington, Virginia

He saw his own name, Lieutenant Colonel Mark "Coolhand" Reynolds written on the subject line of a layered set of papers the clerk handed to him. Mark was standing in the personnel management office of the Secretary of the Air Force on the second floor of the Pentagon. He'd been without a permanent assignment for so long, he'd nearly forgotten whom he worked for, but he was still managed through a personnel system that was designed to groom officers with promising careers.

The papers he held were what Air Force personnel called an RIP. Mark wasn't even sure what the acronym meant, but he did recognize the papers as something he would be required to read through, initial, and sign in a couple of places to acknowledge his acceptance of the assignment identified in the second paragraph.

"Air Attaché, U.S. Embassy, Tel Aviv, Israel," it said. "Report to SAF/IA ASAP."

Mark stood in front of the clerk's desk reading through the forms. He then pulled a pen from the inside pocket of his service dress uniform and hastily signed all three copies on the page where it said he wasn't going to take a "seven day" option. He laughed to himself - like a "seven day option" was really a choice available to him. He was young for his rank and had service agreement commitments for all of the schools he'd been attending. Mark was a lifer and was beginning to realize he was hanging on the end of someone's puppet strings.

When he handed the forms back to the clerk, she riffled through them, making sure everything was in order. "General Jackson said he needs to see you in his office right away. I'll call him and let him know you're on your way," the clerk said while handing him a set of instructions for finding the general's office in Arlington.

Mark left the Pentagon and headed over to Arlington on the Metro. He got off at the Rosslyn stop and walked up Wilson Boulevard where he handed the security personnel on the first floor a memo provided by the Pentagon clerk, stating the purpose of his visit. He handed over his military identification in exchange for a security access badge.

On the eighth floor, Mark was led into a large, wood-paneled office with a picture window that overlooked Alexandria and the

Potomac River. General Jackson's designation of SAF/IA stood for Chief of Secretary of the Air Force's International Airman Program. The General was responsible for recruiting human intelligence personnel for the Defense Intelligence Agency. When Mark entered his office, the General stepped around his desk to shake hands with the new recruit and welcomed him into the program.

"You're going to love Tel Aviv," he said. "That's where I spent my first tour as an attaché and would trade anything to get back there."

Mark had never thought about the kinds of postings that awaited officers who found themselves outside of the main stream. He was adjusting to the idea that his flying career was over and that his dreams of commanding a flying squadron went along with it. At the same time, he thought, *this gig to the Middle East might not be too bad.*

"Normally, we have a vetting and interview process for our attaché candidates. In your case, I had that waived. I have it on good authority that you're a perfect fit for the position. You'll have to attend some language training and then the DIA School for military diplomats before heading over. We'll meet again before you leave the U.S. In the meantime, Edward will provide you with the information you'll need to get started with the required training. Questions?" The General didn't expect Mark to answer and was somewhat taken aback when he did.

"Sir, why me?"

General Jackson let out a hiss of air, then looked at the former combat pilot and said, "I had it on good authority that you would do an excellent job. Working out of the embassy in Tel Aviv is a tricky business. Your record suggests you've got some expertise with UAVs. The Israeli's have been using them in combat operations for quite some time. We need someone with your talent to keep an eye on things for us. Nothing more."

Mark thanked the General and headed down the hall to the man named Edward. Drones. He should have known. He was certain Snake was somehow involved. Mark was pretty sure that before departing for Israel, he'd be meeting up with Randy "Snake" Wormwood again. It irked him that Snake might be thinking he could get what he wanted from Mark.

Mark spent the next eight months at the State Department's Foreign Service Institute learning Hebrew. New Foreign Service Officers normally required one year of language training before heading to post, but for Defense Department Attachés, the only requirement was a sufficient amount of fluency for daily conversation and the ability to read local journals in the target country.

Mark enjoyed the distraction of the one-on-one training and felt comfortable enough with the language before the course concluded. On his third day in the diplomat course, Mark ran into Rachel Jennings. He noticed her when she entered the school's main lecture hall and took a seat in the back corner. At the midday break from the indoctrination briefings that all new diplomats, and in some cases, their wives, received, Mark maneuvered over to Rachel, catching her just as she swiped her security badge to gain access to the staff offices.

"So, this is where you work?" he asked.

"You caught me."

"I mean, really, you work here in human Intel? What are you, an instructor or support staff or something?" he asked. Then, he noticed the quirky, tired look that was Rachel's defining feature. He looked down at her left hand and noticed there was still no wedding ring.

"Something like that, yes. My duties here don't carry much of a job description," she said.

"Well, then, how about lunch? We can catch up. You can give me all the ins and outs of the training," Mark didn't know anybody at the school yet. He'd been so isolated over the past couple of years and with the language training, it was as if he were no longer in the Air Force. He figured Rachel to be a loner just as she was when he met her the first time and wondered if anything had changed for her.

"I don't date students," declared Rachel.

Mark was taken aback and gave her a gasp and a sarcastic grin, intending to convey he couldn't believe what she just said. Then, he decided to inject a bit of humor, "I'll bet you say that to all the gentlemen."

His comment got a rise out of her and for a brief moment she looked less tired and worn out. "Maybe another time, Colonel. I've got pasta waiting on my desk and some work left undone that needs attending to. See you in class," she said as she swiped her badge and slipped through the door to the staff offices.

Mark took the thirteen-week course in stride. There was training on everything from formal dining, to which of his coat pockets are best to carry his business cards, and which ones are best to store those given to him during a cocktail party. There were practical exercises that included weapons training and defensive driving. None of it was new to Mark. Near the end of the course there were the classified briefings and the security and warning briefings about how best to avoid disclosing critical mission details.

CHAPTER 15

Fall 2010 - Tel Aviv, Israel

For Mark Reynolds, the first year at the U.S. Embassy in Tel Aviv was full of activity. True to Major General Jackson's rationale for recruiting him for the position, there was a great deal of Israeli Aerospace Industry devoted to the development and fielding of UAV systems. Mark frequently found himself at cocktail parties and beach picnics, leaving with invitations to tour various drone manufacturing and development facilities.

Although he didn't like the game very much, Mark spent a couple of afternoons on the tennis court. At one of the picnics he'd attended, he met up with an Israeli Army Colonel who hinted at plans to stop progress on a uranium enrichment program in Iran. Mark had learned to elicit information without prying and managed to find out that the Israeli Army Colonel had a passion for tennis.

Mark enjoyed the exercise and found the climate in Tel Aviv to be suitable for year-round enjoyment of outdoor sports. Having beaten the Army Colonel on a few occasions, it was hard for him to avoid being challenged for a rematch. When they finished their latest match, Colonel Gidon Jessup was pleased with himself for having taken the American down in two straight sets, so he offered Mark an invitation to join him in a celebratory cocktail later in the evening.

"I'll send a driver to pick you up. I know the perfect place in Haifa, near to the sea. You'll love the scenery," the Colonel told him.

"Thank you, sir, I'll look forward to it," Mark replied.

The evening was warm for late fall. During his first year in Israel, Mark came to realize there were only two seasons in the East Mediterranean, Summer and Winter. Winter, he decided, was a lot like summer with the exception of a few rainy days and some cold mornings.

When Mark was delivered to the seaside bistro along the waterfront of the old Haifa Harbor, he realized what the Colonel was really saying about the scenery. The promenade in Haifa was like a runway for fashion models. Mark saw Colonel Jessup seated at a table close to the low sea wall. With him were two young women, both dressed in eye-catching summer wear. One blonde and the other brunette, both wearing strappy, heeled sandals and sundresses of light fabric that left little to the imagination. The women were sipping white wine from oversized, stemmed glasses, and the Colonel was swirling a tumbler of scotch.

"Please, have a seat. Mark, I'd like you to meet Rina and Siva," said the Colonel, as if he were showcasing his trophies.

"It is my pleasure," Mark said, taking the empty seat at the table.

"Order what you like," the Colonel said, snapping his hand above his head to get the attention of a waiter who'd already been handsomely tipped. "Siva is, as you might have already guessed, a fashion model." Mark looked in her direction, "Yes, I can see." Then, he turned to Rina, "I suspect perhaps you are also a model?"

"No, Colonel, I'm more of a traditional merchant here in the Levant. I run a gallery in the north of town. Tel Aviv, not here in Haifa. If you have occasion to visit, I will show you the best local art 'Telehket' has to offer."

"Telehket?" Mark asked.

"Yes, the name of the gallery. It stands for the color blue."

The small talk wasn't too excruciating and the evening was enjoyable enough. Neither of the women had much else to say all evening. Most of the conversation was driven by the Colonel, who reminisced of the days of his childhood during the six-day war. He was still too young during the Yum Kippur conflict to don a uniform and fight. His exploits occurred later when the information that he and his small team gathered from covert operations in Iraq resulted in his country's victorious destruction of Iraq's Osirak Nuclear Research Facility.

Through the winter months and into spring, Mark engaged in the repetitious pattern of tennis matches, celebratory cocktails and meals with Jessup. There were always young women involved.

"Mark, why is it that you always leave me to deal with two women at once. The reason I invite two is so that you never have to return to your quarters alone. Then, how do you thank me?" Jessup asked with a hand gesture of exasperation. "By leaving me with not one, but two guests to satisfy for the evening." Jessup was probing Mark and making a joke of it at the same time.

"Sir, I never mix business with pleasure," Mark said. "It is fortuitous that your country is populated with plenty of beautiful women. Please, don't think that I spend my evenings alone as it would be a shame to imagine missing the opportunity to become more friendly with so many lovely women."

The Colonel gave Mark's comment a nod of approval, "as you wish, my friend."

For once, Mark felt like he wasn't actually lying. He had a visitor waiting for him in his quarters. During his time working as an attaché, Mark had grown used to surprises. When he got word that Rachel Jennings wanted a debrief from him on his relations with Jessup, he wasn't surprised at all. With his recollections from the encounters he had in D.C. with Jennings and Snake, he put two and two together and figured the two of them were on some sort of "drone quest," seeking to learn anything they could about Israel's use of the robotic aircraft.

Through this unusual relationship with the older Israeli, Mark had the good fortune to come into contact with officials from the Israeli Aircraft Industries. IAI was working on stealth drone development. He saw a demonstration of the Harpi II vehicle and was shocked that the design was a scaled down version of the vehicle U.S. Manufactures developed for the JUCAS program. There was no doubt in his mind that there was collaboration between the two programs.

When Mark unlocked the door to his elaborately appointed diplomat quarters, he was surprised to see Ms. Jennings seated on his sofa waiting for his return. He'd heard from a colleague at the embassy that someone from the DIA needed to get an update from him on Jessup's activities. He didn't anticipate his contact would be with Rachel Jennings.

"Miss Jennings, it has been a while. How long will you be here in Tel Aviv?" he asked.

"Has it been that long? It's 'Rachel,' I thought we were on a first name basis. Anyway, I can't stay. I'm leaving first thing in the morning, making my rounds to a few of the other posts in the region."

"Okay ,then, we'll have to make the best of our time. Might I suggest we take a walk. I know of a place we can get a drink. We can chat along the way," he made a hand gesture toward his ear and then the rest of the room, indicating to Rachel that he'd discovered his quarters were probably bugged.

"Good idea, it was a long trip," she said.

Mark made a move for the door and waited as Rachel gathered her sweater and a small handbag that matched her outfit. Outside on the sidewalk, as they made their way to a noisy cocktail lounge down near the beach promenade, Mark filled her in on his latest outing with Jessup and his women.

Rachel didn't say anything as he replayed the day's events. He told her all about Jessup and his women over the evening meal. He provided every detail, including how they were dressed and what he could remember about where they lived and worked. At the mention of Rina's name, Rachel asked him for more information, perhaps to confirm her identity. Mark wasn't really sure, but was puzzled by Rachel's reaction.

"You know this woman named Rina?" he asked, waiting for an answer.

Rachel didn't respond. Mark noticed tears pooling in her eyes and decided it would be best not to go any deeper.

"Did you come straight from D.C., or did you get to stop off anywhere on your way out here?" he asked, changing the subject in an attempt to lighten the mood.

"I made a quick stop in Paris. It starts to get a bit chilly there this time of year. I'll admit, I don't mind visiting our embassy there. It's the kind of place that makes a person feel important."

Mark couldn't help notice Rachel's mood change. It seemed like she was clamming up, which he thought was unusual for someone in her line of work.

"Where are you staying?" he asked.

"The Holiday Inn on the beach."

"It's not far, if we're done here, I'll walk you back."

He waited as she slid back from the small bistro table. He left enough cash to cover the bill for their coffee and offered his arm to Rachel as she stepped around the table while they made their exit.

Mark was ready to leave her at the lobby and make his way back to his apartment to turn in early. When Rachel asked him to come up for a night cap, he thought he should, just in case there was something more she needed to share with him.

There was. Mark didn't expect it, but once inside the luxurious suite, she couldn't suppress her sobs or hold back the tears any longer. "Just hold me," she demanded. And he did, until her alarm rang in the early hours. When he awoke, she was gone.

***

As the year was coming to a close, Lieutenant Colonel Mark Reynolds was summoned to the office of the U.S. Ambassador, located in the same building as his office, only it was on the top floor, above the Defense Attaché Offices and the CIA Station Chief's primary location.

When the Ambassador shook Mark's hand, he presented him with a small, felt-lined wooden box. When he opened it, Mark was rewarded with a pair of sterling silver "eagles." The small box contained the rank insignia of full Colonel.

"You probably knew this was coming," the Ambassador said to him, "I'm frocking you. The Defense Attaché has been called away and won't be returning. Since we verified with your service that you now have a line number to the next rank, I've decided that as my new Defense Attaché, you'll need an appropriate rank to operate in that capacity."

Mark came to attention and saluted the Ambassador as he would have had he been standing before the Commander in Chief himself. He shook hands with the senior official and said, "Thank you, sir, I'll give you my best work. You can be sure of it."

"I've no doubt," said the Ambassador as he poured two shots of twenty-year-old scotch from a cut crystal decanter kept on a tray against the walnut-paneled wall of his elaborately decorated office.

CHAPTER 16

Fall 2011 - Natanz, Iran

Reza was very happy when he opened the small gift from Heydar.

"A runner's watch. How did you know I'd appreciate such a gift?" Reza asked his friend.

"It has all the latest features. There is enough memory to store data from several runs so that you can compare performances. It even gathers heart rate information. Here, let me show you." Reza paid close attention to Heydar and listened.

"This patch near the plastic clasp is a sensor that reads your pulse. Watch this," Heydar said while he pressed the watchband against the inside of his wrist and the symbology on the watch face registered his pulse. "It isn't something that you'd look at while you're running, but it could be useful during interval training and comparing heart-rate data to kilometer splits," he said.

"Thank you. Thank you so much for thinking of me on my birthday. Even Termeh wouldn't know that I'd appreciate such a gift. I only wish that it were this year that we'll be going to New York to run the marathon there."

"Next year. We'll make it happen next year. We can prepare our minds by going for a long run on the same day as the New York Marathon, then we can stay up late and watch the start together on the television," offered Heydar.

"I like that idea," Reza said. "It is a good thing the event is on a Saturday this year. Otherwise, I'm not sure I'd be able to take off from work."

"Things are going better for you these days?" asked Heydar.

"Swimmingly," said Reza, using an expression he'd heard from another engineer who'd just returned from a visit to the United States. "Thank you again for the watch, Heydar. I'll wear it always and by next year, we'll be comparing data when we finish the New York Marathon."

Reza thought the watch Heydar gave him must be the newest Timex. It was a version of the "Iron Man" Timex, but instead of the menu being geared toward Triathlons, this new variation was specifically designed for the marathon runner.

***

The early morning air was crisp, which felt good to Reza. He just finished one of his easy, six-mile runs. He ran his easy workouts on alternating days and the more difficult workouts in the evenings with Heydar. It gave him a chance to learn how to use some of the data from his new watch. He'd cycle through the menus when he finished his runs, then review and record them after he'd settled into the morning routines at his office.

Reza didn't think about whether he should remove the watch along with his wallet and keys from his pockets when he went through the security gauntlet at the Natanz facility. In fact, he'd completely forgotten he had it on. Since it was made almost entirely of plastic, the material provided natural insulation for the small amounts of gold SMT wire within, so Reza didn't set off the metal detection screen even though he still wore his watch.

When he sat down at his desk and logged into his desktop computer, the black terminal window opened briefly, acknowledging it was Reza's work station that was pinging the closed network connected to the central controls responsible for maintaining the health and welfare of the centrifuges. He didn't notice that an extra line of code flashed at the end of each of the log in routines. After all, the terminal screen was only visible for less than about five seconds and the automated lines of instructional code flashed by so fast that one would have to had a reason to look. The terminal screen would have offered an opportunity for a forensic analysis of everything within the network, but the malware was pretty elegant. It had a looping routine that prevented anomalies from showing up during the booting or rebooting processes.

While he was waiting for the rest of his email to download, Reza removed the Timex and pressed one of the buttons several times, cycling through the data he collected during his morning run. Satisfied that he was improving his training results over the previous week, he strapped it back on his wrist and went to work reviewing the status of Iran's most hopeful U-235 production. He thought to himself how pleased the authorities at the Atomic Energy Organization of Iran would be when they found out that the materials would be ready for testing and use before the year was out.

Reza was so focused on his version of a future Iran, that he allowed himself to ignore the reasons various agencies within the Iranian government started to show more interest in his work. He never really paid attention to the possibility that others in Iran were more interested in using the materials to build a warhead that could ride atop a Shahab-3 liquid-fueled or the newer solid fuel Sajjil-2 missile.

Technical experts from both the Ministry of Intelligence and National Security of the Islamic Republic of Iran known as MISIRI, along with others from the Cyber Police under the Army of the Guardians of the Islamic Revolution, made regular visits to the facility. Reza didn't have any idea who these people were or what their purpose was, nor did he care.

At the conclusion of his workday at Natanz, Reza drove back to his home in Isfahan and was relieved to be working from his nearby office for the remainder of the week. Before Termeh arrived home from her work at the university hospital, Reza prepared his morning workout plan so that when he met up with Heydar for a session on the university track, he'd be ready.

He opened his laptop and logged onto the Internet. He pulled up a web-based program used to store his daily statistics which allowed him to compare training results with other participants in the online running and training club. Reza was completely oblivious to the interaction taking place between his Timex and the laptop. Unbeknown to him, a packet of coded command and control software made its way into the ether of the Internet.

Reza met with Heydar the following evening just outside of the university stadium for their evening run on the track.

Their workout was intense. After ten repeat 400s at seventy seconds each, they finished the evening with an easy mile around the track. It took a couple of laps before either of them was able to speak comfortably.

"That was amazing, Reza. The best workout in months!" Heydar exclaimed.

"We'll have to remember this one next year when we train for

New York."

"Let's imagine that we'll be there in two weeks. We can run our own marathon here in Isfahan. Just the two of us, a week from Saturday," said Heydar with genuine enthusiasm.

"Okay, it is settled. We can use some of the course that we measured on our bicycles for our long runs. The rest we'll have to map out, but I think we could maybe just loop some of the original nineteen-mile route we did two weeks ago," Reza said with some excitement.

"These next ten days we taper," said Heydar.

"Okay, we can confirm the exact distance of the route this Saturday on our bikes so that next week…yes, we'll be New York Marathon finishers even before the starting gun sounds."

On the day of the New York Marathon, six hours before the race started in New York, Reza and Heydar were on the road running the route they'd both worked out to complete exactly 26.2 miles at the point where they entered the University of Isfahan stadium, crossing over a line painted on the middle of the track.

After Reza and Heydar completed their marathon, they went to Reza's home in Isfahan to watch the New York City Marathon on television. Instead of enjoying the afterglow of having completed the 26.2 miles earlier in the day, Reza was met by his wife, Termeh, bearing urgent news when he walked through the door.

"It is Saturday, Termeh, I don't need to call the facility manager on my day off. It can wait until tomorrow," said Reza.

"I don't think that is a good idea. They said something has happened in Natanz and you need to contact them right away."

"Okay, I'm sorry Termeh. I didn't mean to blare anger at the messenger," Reza said to his wife, stroking her gently on the shoulder. "I'll call them back right away." Then, he turned to his friend. "Heydar, I'm sorry. You'd better go watch the marathon at your own place. I'm afraid whatever is happening with my work is going to keep me for quite a while."

"No problem, my friend. I'll record it and we can watch together at another time. I hope things turn out alright with your work. Let me know if there is anything I can do," Heydar said, and waved a goodbye and thanked Termeh.

Reza never saw his friend Heydar again.

CHAPTER 17

November 2011 - Tel Aviv, Israel

The morning was crisp and cool, so Mark Reynolds pulled on a sweat suit over his tennis attire. He grabbed his sport duffle containing the three Wilson K Tour 90 rackets, just like the ones Roger Federer used to win so many championships. Mark's game had improved substantially since taking up the friendly competition with his Israeli counterpart, Gidon Jessup.

Their routine was relatively the same. Every other week, they'd meet on a Saturday morning for a light breakfast, then Jessup would have his driver deliver them to a different country club. One of the luxuries a man like Jessup who'd recently been promoted to Brigadier General had access to was cooperation from those beholden to Israel's defense industry. Many of the country club owners were beneficiaries of the wealthy members from the defense industry's private sector and knew General

Jessup well, so they kept their doors open to him as a professional courtesy.

Today's outing took them on a forty-minute drive north to a quaint country club with courts positioned high up on the cliffs in the small town of Caesarea.

"It is impossible to enjoy a good game of tennis here at any other time of the year," said Jessup. "In summer, by nine in the morning the wind becomes too strong and doesn't let up until well after dark. Any later into the winter and there is a morning frost. There are better places to play where it isn't so cold, but on a day like today?"

"It sure is a beautiful spot," Mark said, looking around at the view.

"Right, then, let's get down to it, shall we?" Jessup suggested.

Going into the third set, Mark was exhausted but glad for the cool, fall morning air. He decided not to hold back and took Jessup in sudden death after being tied in the final set. It was mid-day before they finished, and both of them were too fatigued from the excitement of the match to engage in conversation right away. Mark shook Jessup's hand and thanked him for the match.

On the ride back to Tel Aviv Jessup said, "You know, I think you played very well today. I wasn't up to form as I'd hoped, but next time, you will see. I think you may have been practicing in secret. Your backhand down the line shot, I have never seen you use it until today. After you clinched the first set with that shot, I thought it might have been a fluke, but you proved otherwise."

"I got lucky," Mark said.

"More than once today," replied Jessup with a sly grin. "I have a special treat for this evening's celebratory meal."

"No, you mustn't," Mark said and really meant it.

"I insist. You cannot beat me in a match as you have today without meeting the terms of our agreement. You win, you buy me dinner, I win and the tables turn. Same as always."

The conversation ended as Jessup's driver pulled up alongside the curb of Mark's apartment complex near Embassy Row in downtown Tel Aviv.

"I'll have you picked up at six right here. Then, we'll enjoy a special evening. Wear something warm, we'll be on the terrace for cocktails," Jessup told him, just before instructing his driver to pull away.

Mark wasn't thrilled about going through the motions he'd become accustomed to every time he met Jessup for a meal. It was always the same. The older man looked relaxed as though he'd been living the highlife. It was as though he'd always had two lovely, nameless women in his presence, one on each arm. They were like jewelry to the Israeli general and Mark couldn't figure out where he had the time to meet all of them, since during each encounter Jessup had different girls.

He once told Mark that he went to a lot of dinner and cocktail parties hosted by Defense Industrial Partners. "These girls are not what you might think, my friend," he said to Mark. "Tell me you'd never suspect that I'd pay for call girls or escorts, hmmm? No, my friend, as you probably have the same in the United States, we have our share of 'gold diggers' here in my country as well. I don't mind, really. They have a good time and I don't give them any encouragement. I wouldn't want them to think I might someday become the marrying kind of guy. No, I think they gravitate my way as a challenge."

At six p.m. sharp, Mark stood in front of the entry to his apartment complex waiting for Jessup's driver coming to pick him up. He wore a long-sleeved cardigan beneath a suede, leather coat for warmth. Casual slacks and loafers completed his get up. Mark never wore anything elaborate. He didn't want to draw more attention than the average male his age does on the streets of Tel Aviv. The one exception to this way of thinking was the heavy, stainless bezel Rolex Submariner he wore beneath the sleeve of his jacket.

The evening turned out just as Mark had anticipated. He played through every prompt of their established pattern. Meeting the young women who made Jessup feel like a younger man. Commenting on the quality of food and complimenting the wait staff as though Jessup's choice of dining venues were an achievement. All of it would soon culminate as it always had on such occasions, with Jessup leaving with the two women and Mark returning to his Tel Aviv apartment alone.

However, on this particular evening, everything changed in an instant. With a blinding flash, loud noise and screams came from every direction, and pieces of metal and glass flew into the air along with the exploding vehicle. In the confusion, Mark wasn't sure what was causing him to become so disoriented. He couldn't detect any physical injury. It was his last conscious thought.

CHAPTER 18

November 2011 - North Arlington, Virginia

Snake waited patiently in his luxurious office, covertly situated within the walls of an aging concrete building lacking any architectural or esthetic value - making it a perfect location for a CIA Detachment. The basement of the building housed a scaled down version of a Remote Signals Intercept Operations Center, fed by an elaborate network of RF feeds from remote antennas used to transmit and receive with terrestrial and satellite communications gear. The network also consisted of hardened T-1 data lines.

A buzz on the intercom that sat on Snake's desk broke him from a spell of contemplation. He'd been thinking of the possible next steps depending on the outcome of the operation he was overseeing.

"This is Wormwood, what is it," he answered into the

intercom.

"I just got a call from downstairs, sir, they are ready for you," his office assistant said. Wormwood referred to Ms. Melanie Murphy as his "Moat Dragon." Nobody was allowed to contact him or bother him without going through her first.

"The best moat dragon in the business!" boasted Wormwood at Ms. Murphy's recognition ceremony for twenty years of service.

"Tell them I'm on my way down. Thanks, Mel," he replied.

He took the stairs two at a time, and when he arrived at the secure door that led into the ops center, a fresh-faced young man wearing dress slacks and pressed shirt and tie, held the door open for him.

"Thanks, Jimmy. What have we got?" Snake asked the young operations watch chief.

"Sir, overhead has some confirmation, and we're getting reports from sources in Tehran that something devastating happened to the target in Natanz." Jimmy led Snake over to a console where he was able to view a live motion IR feed from a DoD satellite in Low Earth Orbit. This particular bird was equipped with hyper-spectral sensors. The observer could view the images during a live pass, but the collected images over time were then fed into an imagery database, and a software routine re-constructed the scenes designated by the user to provide a complete chronology.

Using change detection technologies, the user can watch the entire story unfold and see what it looked like when the nuclear enrichment facility housing the daisy chains of centrifuges imploded.

Drawing Snakes attention to the terminal, Jimmy said, "Sir, the pass in these low orbits happened pretty fast, but I think you'll appreciate the way the oblique angles provide some perspective of the damage."

The satellite's imagery sensor was programmed to stare at the center of the facility throughout the pass. Snake watched the feed intently, which took just under four minutes. "What were those orange and blue signatures? They look like they are glowing."

"Not what you might think, sir. It will be another twenty-three and a half minutes before we get another pass, so let me show you something that might explain what you just saw a little bit better."

Jimmy scrolled the curser around on the SunSpark Micro System display and clicked on a file icon that was continuously being fed and updated. What Snake was treated to next was a movie of the Natanz facility going through the last throes of its operational life. The violence was evident, even at an orbit range of 275 kilometers.

"So, you can confirm the destruction we just witnessed is total?"

"No, sir, but I can confirm that it was effective. Our sources inside Tehran are reporting that officials at the Islamic Republic of Iran's Atomic Energy Organization are in a tizzy about the setbacks these events caused to their program."

"Any reports on the status in Natanz? Fallout, nuclear or otherwise?"

"Nothing yet, sir."

"Alright then, we need to clean our tracks. Let's get rid of the source and every agent we know of whom our source had contact with."

Snake saw the look on Jimmy's face and noticed the heads of every agent in the ops center turning in his direction when he issued his instructions.

"I know what all of you might be thinking, and yes, there will be some collateral damage and maybe even fratricide, but this operation was big. Eyes on from the very top and WE, ladies and gentlemen, succeeded with this stage of the mission. Now, we have to make sure there is no trace or possibility of anyone ever finding out how it was done. Remember, we want to be able to come back and do it again in a couple of years."

Snake turned to leave the ops room. The crew swiveled their chairs back around and returned to their work while Jimmy held the door open for his director's exit.

On his way back up the steps, Snake imagined how the next stage of the operation would go down. He reminded himself that he was the only one in contact with Marios, which meant he'd have to find a way to take care of his end of the cover up. When he arrived back in his office, Melanie stopped him.

"Better not go in there, sir, I just got another call from downstairs."

Snake Wormwood shook his head, "I'm needed down there again?"

"Yes, sir."

Jimmy was holding the door open for him when he returned to the ops center. "Sir, we lost track of one of the sources."

"Which one?"

"The main one in Iran. Sorry, sir, we never found out from him who he was running inside the facility. The man's name is Heydar, and we think he was silenced before we could find out."

"You think? Jimmy, we need to know precisely. With the big hairy eyeballs on this operation, there can be no mistakes. We need ground truth, okay?"

"Sir, these things normally take some time."

"We can't afford that kind of time in a situation like this," Wormwood said in a low tone, trying not to sound like there was blame to lay on his crew. After all, they did what he ordered them to do. "We'll have to make some adjustments to our plan on the fly. Have we executed the operations against the sources in Israel yet?"

"Not yet, sir."

"Okay, we'll move out on that one right away, but make sure Coolhand survives. I want him under our complete control. We may need him to help us unravel this thing, but we can't allow any leaks. Just get him back here soonest."

CHAPTER 19

5 December 2011 - Bethesda Naval Hospital Ward 8

Coolhand made a quick survey of the corridor, checking a reflection in the glass door to make sure the orderly wouldn't notice he was heading directly to a set of glass doors at the opposite end that opened to a staff parking area and access road. Coolhand hoped the foil patch he was using to cover the implant would be sufficient to prevent tracking. He had no way of knowing for sure. He figured he'd find out soon enough.

Once outside of the building, he stood beneath an awning waiting for young Ronny Clark and his cousin to spot him. He was pretty confident the young Marine would be true to his word. He didn't have to wait long, which was a good thing because the outside air temperature was hovering in the mid-teens. He spotted the unmistakable profile of the young jarhead sitting in the passenger seat of a dark, metallic-green 1970 GTO. Coolhand could tell the driver was equally young and noted the familial relationship in the shape of his forehead. Just like Corporal Ronny Clark's.

The GTO pulled up and Ronny got out to let the Colonel climb in. He stood holding the door and paused, at a loss for what he should do next.

"Sir?" Ronny reached to shake hands with the Colonel, then reached up with his other hand to scratch his head, looking back at the two-door muscle car.

"Ronny, thanks. I'll just jump in back," Coolhand said, patting the Marine on the shoulder. He also noticed Ronny's expression of relief when he let him off the hook with respect to military protocol. He really didn't want Ronny to give up the front seat to him while his cousin drove them away.

They turned away from the medical facility's gate and headed north on the boulevard and onto the Washington Parkway toward Baltimore.

"Guys, thanks for doing this. It's nice to get out," Coolhand said.

"My pleasure, sir. Any friend of Ronny, here, is a friend of mine. Where to? Oh, and my name is Bobby," Ronny's cousin said over his shoulder as he merged onto the two-lane highway.

"Depends," said Coolhand. "Where are you guys headed?"

"Bobby lives just north of Fort Meade. His wife works there, at NSA, I mean. Hey, I'll bet she could arrange for you to use an office with a DSN to make those calls we talked about," Ronny offered.

"How about this, let me out just up here at this off-ramp leading to that strip mall. I can make all the necessary calls on a commercial line. Don't you worry Ronny, I've got your back, and Bobby, you need to get your cousin started on a little R and R anyway. I'm a big boy, I'll make my calls, wander around a bit and take a cab back to Bethesda. If we go much farther, that cab fare is gonna gouge the hell out of my wallet," Coolhand told them.

"Okay, sir, you've got it." Bobby took the exit ramp and pulled into a sparsely occupied parking area in front of a handful of commercial establishments. There were no phone booths in sight.

"Tell you what, guys, this will work just fine. I'll head over to that pool hall over there. If they don't have a payphone, I'm sure they'd let me use a house phone so long as I start a tab with my credit card."

Ronny handed Coolhand a copy of his assignment and release paper, containing all the information a good commander would need to execute a personnel action. Coolhand took a look at the print out and then back into the eyes of the young Marine. He shook hands with both the young men, then turned to Bobby and said, "Take care of this warrior for us. He's one of the good ones." Then, he turned to Ronny again, giving the Marine a light tap on his shoulder with a closed fist and said, "Don't worry, everything is going to be just fine." Coolhand slipped out of the backseat from behind Ronny and jumped out of the GTO, high-tailing into the pool hall to get out of the cold.

The glass door swung shut behind him, and as he shrugged his shoulders to shake off the cold and looked over back outside, he noticed the GTO speeding out of the parking area and back onto the access road leading to the highway. *Damn good people, and damn good kid*, he thought as he entered the pool hall. Coolhand didn't have a credit card on him and had no intention of calling anyone on Ronny's behalf. The kid will just have to fend for himself. Coolhand rationalized that Ronny was no worse off than he would have been even if he didn't offer to make that call for him.

Coolhand knew that a man in a uniform covered by a subdued, camouflaged winter overcoat and stocking cap wasn't always a rare sight in the Washington D.C. region, especially after 9-11. Before then, there were protocols for uniform wear all over the country based on what command a military member was assigned and which state they were in. There was a regulation for everything before the two towers came down. After that, the military culture in the homeland called for all service members to wear combat dress as their uniform of the day.

Coolhand didn't see a payphone anywhere nearby, so he asked to use the house phone. The proprietor didn't seem at all phased by Coolhand's battle dress fatigues. Before he dialed, he gave a brief thought to the breach of trust he committed between himself and the young Marine.

"Sorry, Ronny, I don't know anybody that can improve your situation. You're on your own now, and you'll be better off for it," Coolhand whispered to himself.

He punched in a number that was etched permanently in his mind. The number he entered was one no mental torture could erase from his memory, It remained the lifeline to his former life with his ex-wife and two daughters.

He called Anne while imagining that she'd had sufficient time to get back from dropping the girls off at school with her morning errands already complete. Charles would have been at his office on the waterfront overlooking the Baltimore Harbor, maybe in his conference room defending a small-time importer's business from tax vultures.

"Hello," Anne said, short of breath.

There was a long pause. She said again, "Hello, can you hear me?" she asked, sounding less distracted.

"Anne, I'm sorry to bother you like this," Mark finally said.

She didn't say anything and the line was an open hiss.

"Anne, it's me, Mark. Really, I'm sorry to call you like this, but I need a favor."

Again, his ex didn't reply. Nothing but the hiss of an open line was heard on Mark's end. "Anne, Anne, are you there?"

"Mark, if that is really you, yes, I'm here."

He heard the sound coming from the other end of the line that sounded like a gasp. Mark waited through the long, dead pause on the line, then detected what sounded like sobbing on the other end. "Whatever it is, Anne, I can explain. Can we meet somewhere? I could really use your help right now, then I promise, I'll leave you and the girls alone."

After hanging up the phone, Mark waited twenty minutes, sipping from a cup of black coffee before he saw his ex-wife pull up in front of the pool hall with the family Subaru wagon. He set the cup down, along with some cash, then dashed through the cold of the outdoor air to join his ex in the warmth of her vehicle. He could tell she'd been crying.

"What is it?" he asked.

Anne didn't answer. She reached around between the seats and retrieved her satchel containing journals and her notebook. From it, she pulled out a newspaper from the previous week. On the second page of the A-section of the Washington Times was a small column that covered a minor car-bombing event in Haifa Israel. The lead line read, "U.S. Diplomat Killed in Car Bombing."

Mark read the three paragraphs that only contained presumably known facts about the event. The article was inconclusive as to a motive and there was no organization claiming responsibility. The article went on to say that there were two other victims, including an Israeli Army General and a woman.

His memories weren't exactly flooding back after reading the article, but the pieces were falling into place. Mark's last memory of his work in Israel was his evening with General Jessup, and he had a vague recollection of an explosion.

"Anne, I'm here, now, alive," he said, looking into her teary eyes.

"I know. I know. It's just…so unbelievable." She took another look at the way he was dressed in military desert battle fatigues with the addition of a black, woolen scarf, gloves and stocking cap. She noted the rank tab bearing the symbol of an eagle near the zipper of his jacket.

"Mark, I haven't seen you in a uniform in years. I didn't think the work you were doing required a uniform. What have you been up to anyway?" she asked.

"Anne, the uniform has nothing to do with anything. It's just clothing," he said. Then, he realized she was right, it was almost as if his presence in the U.S. didn't fit into any version of the actual chronology of his past weeks.

"Really. I just need your help with a few things and then I won't bother you or the girls ever again. Nobody can ever know we saw each other either." He was following his instincts at this point and knew that his family would be in danger if it became known that he'd received assistance from them.

"Anne, do the girls think I'm dead?" he asked with some reservation.

"Yes. Yes, there was a memorial. We all went. Even Charles."

"God, Anne. I'm so sorry. You've got to believe I had no idea. If I'd had any clue, I wouldn't have called."

She drove him to their home in Chevy Chase. "Charles has some clothes that will fit you. Do you need money? Anything? Just tell me what I can do." Mark could tell Anne was confused. The expression she wore revealed she must be torn between a vast choice of emotions. Anger, frustration, remorse, sadness, loss, all of it must have flooded in at once.

"Thanks, Anne, I'll be away as soon as possible. I'll disappear. Tell the girls I'm in heaven saving a place for all of us. Even Charles. He's a good man and he's lucky to have you. Thank you again for everything."

Mark tucked the Pendleton scarf into the heavy, camel-hair coat Anne found for him. The slacks and turtleneck were heavy enough to ward off some of the cold, too. Earlier, while Mark was changing into the clothes his ex commandeered for him, she went upstairs to the study she shared with Charles and returned with a small, vinyl wallet that looked like it came from a bank. As he was preparing to leave, she handed it to him with tears streaming from her eyes.

"SGLI paid a large sum of tax-free dollars into my personal account last week. Charles doesn't know anything about it. I didn't know what to do, so I opened a separate account under my maiden name with the idea this money would set the girls up for a good education and then some. Mark, we don't need any of it. Charles already set up an education fund for them. As far as I'm concerned, none of this should have ever happened. I'm just glad you're alive. I know I shouldn't ask, so I won't. Just take it and go somewhere safe."

Mark knew his ex had spent enough time in his world to know that whatever twisted events led him back to the United States in the form of a ghost, probably wouldn't keep his family safe if anyone ever found out he'd contacted any of them.

"You can't take out more than $500 at a time using an ATM and only three withdrawals in a day. I didn't write down the Pin anywhere. It's the same one we used to use before…before we split." He figured she wanted to say, "before you left," but knew it wasn't true. They'd had years of distance between them before the divorce. They never spoke of who bore most the blame, but he knew it wasn't in her nature to cause anymore hurt.

Mark held both her shoulders in his palms, leaned in and kissed her forehead. "Keep the girls safe. Forget I ever came here and please, rest assured I'll find a way to make it up to you."

He pocketed the debit card in its vinyl wallet, turned and

strode away from the fine suburban home that Charles had bought for the family he'd left behind.

CHAPTER 20

7 December 2011 - Baltimore, Maryland

The first thing Mark did after leaving his ex's suburban home in a taxicab was to hit up an ATM at the bus station near Chevy Chase. After the machine coughed out five sets of twenties amounting to $500, Mark waited for the confirmation receipt so that he knew what he'd be working with. Not surprising, he discovered Anne was true to her word and what remained in the account was $399,500.00. She'd deposited the entire $400K from the Serviceman's Group Life Insurance. He could have made his daughters the beneficiaries, but it would have involved setting up a trust. Now, he was glad he never took the time for that chore.

He bought himself a bus ticket to Baltimore where he checked into a Super-8 hotel after stopping in at a Walgreens Drug Store to pick up a few things he knew he needed. The hotel wasn't far from the Port of Baltimore. He was thinking of the various avenues available to him for leaving the country without identification or a passport. He figured the port was a good place to start. However, before going further with any more movements, Coolhand's first order of business was to remove the tracking implant from behind his left ear.

Fortunately, the scar from the insertion of the device was still fresh enough that opening the wound and removing the foreign object wouldn't be too difficult. The angles were awkward for Mark, using the mirror while slowly cutting into his scalp with the surgical knife he picked up at the drug store. He also bought rubbing alcohol, and an adventure first-aid kit that included sutures and a curved needle for sewing himself up.

"Damn that freakin hurts," he said aloud after reaching in to pull out the tracking chip. He wasn't sure of the device's capabilities, so instead of flushing it down the toilet, he wrapped it again in several layers of foil and put it away for safe keeping. Stitching himself up wasn't any less painful than removing the chip in the first place, but when Mark was done, he was glad that there was no residual bleeding from the wound. He made himself a bandage and put the stocking cap back on to hold everything in place and cover up the bandage to avoid looking conspicuous.

Coolhand knew he needed to come up with a plan to remain off-grid. Someone within the U.S. Government already helped him to some extent by making his death public and official, as evidenced by the disbursement of the SGLI payment to his ex. He also realized that whoever these people were, they knew he wasn't really dead and for some reason wanted him alive and in their custody.

Sitting on the bed in the hotel room, Coolhand allowed himself the luxury to do some thinking and wracked his brain to recall bits and pieces from his memory. He needed to determine who it was that might have brought him into the center of this bizarre adventure. He took inventory of what he was sure he knew thus far.

First, something happened in Israel that brought him back to the states. Second, the nuclear enrichment program in Iran was interrupted, causing a great deal of damage in Natanz. Third, the Iranians claimed to have shot down an American drone. To confuse matters, or maybe even shed light on them, Coolhand was pretty sure that the Israeli General Jessup was somehow tied to the events. The common thread running through the series of recent events kept leading Coolhand back to Randy "Snake" Wormwood. If Mark hadn't found himself somehow entangled in this mess, he wouldn't be so convinced of Snake's involvement.

He made a cursory assessment of his physical situation, realizing that access to money was going to be important to him, at least for the time being. He also thought about how easily a large sum of money would be tracked. His initial plan involved broad

loadable debit cards. He grabbed ten from the rack. At the cash register, he noticed the quizzical look on the cashier's face when he dumped all ten cards on the counter and pulled out a bunch of bills and paid the $500 to load $50 onto each of the cards.

"Christmas gifts," he said to the cashier.

"Oh. Makes sense," said the cashier. "I didn't think you looked like a drug dealer or money launderer."

"You get that a lot around here?" Mark asked him.

"No, I read a lot of urban fiction and have been writing some of it myself. I wrote a novel last month during the National Novel Writing Month, but it isn't ready. Lots of edits and holes in the story. You buying all these cards just gave me the idea I needed to make some necessary revisions," said the cashier who was dressed like a hipster underneath the apron he wore that brandished the Walgreens colors.

"Glad I could help," Mark said. Then, he left to find another Starbucks where he could finish his little financial management project. When he was finished, each of the cards had $500 on them. Then, he went back to the Super-8 to remove anything that might connect him specifically to his stay at that location, including the tracking chip still wrapped in the foil from the cigarette packs.

The clothing he'd gotten from Charles wasn't fancy but at the same time, he didn't look like a homeless guy. He seemed to blend in. He walked the few blocks over to the Greyhound station where he found what he was looking for.

At the bus depot, he took a look at the schedule and noticed there was a westbound coach heading to Albuquerque. He located the departure bay. The chairs and benches were occupied by those about to board. He found a spot next to a guy who appeared to have had better days in the past. Mark sat down next to him and laid his things down on the bench between them. Rolled up in his jacket was the Acer laptop now containing the chip that once transmitted position data from behind his left ear.

***

While sitting in the men's room stall, Mark reformatted the Acer's hard drive just to be sure, then took the battery out and slipped the chip inside, securing it with a piece of tape so that it wouldn't interfere with anything.

Mark nudged the man sitting on the bench. "Albuquerque?" he asked the scruffy-looking guy.

"Yep. You?"

"Same."

"Hey, could you watch my stuff? I gotta go take care of something. No place in the men's room clean enough to hang my coat if you know what I mean."

"Yeah, sure, man, I gotcha covered," said the guy who looked like he could use a shave.

Perfect, Mark was thinking as he got up and walked around the corner of the terminal. He positioned himself so that he could look up into one of those moon-shaped mirrors up high in a corner, intended to assist security and law enforcement with keeping an eye on things. Mark watched the guy on the bench looking around before lifting the corner of the rolled up jacket. The guy wasn't too good at being discrete either. Apparently he felt the hard shell of the laptop and lifted the jacket up to confirm his good fortune.

The timing was perfect. The coach leaving for Albuquerque just started up and riders were boarding. Mark heard the announcement for final boarding and watched his guy look around for him. He then saw the driver starting to close the door. The guy grabbed Mark's coat and laptop and dashed toward the bus, waving to the driver to let him on. When the bus drove away, Mark was pretty satisfied he'd done something that might buy him enough time to throw any potential pursuers off his trail.

***

LAMB

//FM: H. Smith/field Ops/CIA//
//TO: R. Wormwood/Deputy Director OGA/Mid-East Field Desk//Director SpecWar/DARPA
//SUBJ: TARGET STATUS UPDATE//

A. ARLINTON VIRGINIA (OPS CTR)

1. Target re-acquired- Colonel Reynolds's tracker signal traced to a Greyhound Bus Station in the Baltimore Area. Signal indicates movement over past several hours. Auxiliary team is researching possible reasons for previously lost signal.

2. Reynolds location is now in the region of the I-70 corridor near the Pennsylvania state line. Intercept team has been dispatched.

3. Recommend all parties handle Reynolds with extreme caution. Developments indicate Reynolds's escape from Bethesda's Ward 8 was well planned.

//END OF MSG//

CHAPTER 21

7 December 2011 Isfahan, Iran

In the days following the catastrophe at Natanz, Reza was at a loss for how to spend his time. Everything he'd been working toward over the previous ten years was destroyed. He had no idea what took place to cause such a mess. The saving grace was that no radiation leaked beyond the confines of the actual buildings where the machines had been spinning the uranium.

The day before, an investigator from the Cyber Police wearing the uniform of an army captain with the insignia of the Guardians of the Islamic Republic had been by to visit Reza.

"From what we understand, you don't have many friends and you don't socialize much with the others from AEOI. Your wife is a medical doctor, is this correct?"

"Yes, she's a medical doctor. Both of us work a lot." Reza had a tremendous urge to get out of his office and away from these investigators. He knew what he needed was a vigorous run, only he hadn't seen or heard from Heydar since the day the Natanz facility was destroyed.

"Sir, I'm a runner. That is my thing. When I'm not here or at home, I'm on the road or the track. It pretty much consumes all my spare time."

"You run alone?"

"Not always, no."

"Who are your running partners, then?"

"I haven't seen him in several days, but I run with a man I've known for many years. His name is Heydar, and he's a computer engineer with DP Iran Co." Reza noticed the investigator writing everything down. The investigator seemed satisfied with Reza's cooperation.

"There will probably be other officials coming by to visit and ask questions. Thank you for your patience in this matter. After we find out more about what happened to the facility, I'm guessing you will be very busy getting things up and running again," said the investigator as he left Reza standing alone in his office.

Since it all began, Reza had a small TV in his office with the IRIB broadcasting constantly with breaking news. There was nothing new until later in the afternoon. A breaking story temporarily set Reza's mind at ease. The Air Defense Force of the Islamic Republic was being congratulated for successfully shooting down an American made "stealth combat drone" over the vicinity of Natanz and Isfahan. There were pictures that accompanied the newscast, but no mention of the destruction of Iran's best hope for nuclear energy.

Reza's relief was short-lived. The following morning, two officials from the Ministry of Intelligence and National Security of the Islamic Republic of Iran, better known as MISIRI, came to conduct another interview with Dr. Farrokh Reza Khadem.

"Dr. Khadem, it is a tragedy that so much of your work was ruined. We hope you don't mind the questions. It is necessary for all of us involved to unravel the mystery of what happened here so that we can safely and confidently put our energy program back on track," said the senior intelligence official attempting to sound less threatening.

"I understand completely," Reza said. "I'm happy to help in any way that I can."

"This man who was your running partner," began the other MISIRI official who was a short, intellectual type. Probably spent most of his time doing research and analysis. "He worked at DP Iran Co. Is this correct?"

"Yes. That is what he told me. I've never been to his office, but we had conversations about computing and Heydar wasn't at all secretive about offering advice."

"So, the two of you discussed your work?"

Reza was becoming nervous with the direction and tone the questions were taking, "We ran many miles together. We talked about many things over the years and yes, in general terms, we discussed our work. Nothing in any detail, though. I've been working in secure environments my entire career and would not jeopardize security with respect to my position. I'm a professional," declared Reza.

"We're not questioning your integrity, Dr. Khadem, but we are concerned about your friend, Heydar. Have you seen this man lately?"

"Not since the disaster, no. Why the interest? He's still my friend and if he is in trouble, I would like to know."

"We cannot go into much detail with you, Dr. Khadem, not just yet, but our forensic specialists have discovered some interesting activity within the closed computer network at Natanz. It is probably nothing, but we need to leave no stone unturned. You understand, I'm sure," said the nerdy-looking investigator.

"I think that is all for now, Dr. Khadem," said the taller investigator. The MISIRI official handed Reza a business card and thanked him for his time. "If you think of anything, anything at all that would help with the investigation, give me a call. The sooner we sort through the evidence, the sooner we'll know what broke and you can get back to work on a better system. We heard possibly there were some issues with electromagnetic bearing failure. If that was the case, you should be back to work in no time."

The MISIRI officials left Reza to ponder what was said during the visit. They couldn't possibly know anything about bearing failures. Something else would have had to cause that to happen. Reza became very agitated. He sensed that somehow his relationship with Heydar was connected to last week's catastrophe. The comments about the closed network and forensic analysis had Reza pretty keyed up.

He turned his wrist up to look at his watch, wondering if he had time for a quick run before returning and closing up shop for the day. He knew that a run would do him some good, but when he checked the time, everything clicked into place. His watch! He never took it off and it was the only possible way of infiltrating the network at Natanz. Reza didn't know how it could be possible, but the coincidences were lining up in such a way that he didn't think it could be anything else.

He took the watch that Heydar gave him and removed it from his wrist. His inclination was to take the back off and peek inside, in search of something that shouldn't be there, but decided that with micro nano and surface mount technology applications, he'd have no way to determine if anything was out of place.

Reza knew that the two groups of officials who just paid him a visit would have access to technical experts and equipment that would allow them to examine his watch. He also knew that it would mean they would surmise that it was he who unknowingly introduced something foreign into the command and control network at Natanz. There would be no recovery from such involvement. Reza's heart rate increased at the thought and his skin turned hot.

CHAPTER 22

7 December 2011 - Arlington, Virginia

Snake thought about an important lesson he'd learned early on in his career. "Everyone has a boss!" For Wormwood, this knowledge and awareness was never an impediment since he'd always been afforded the luxury of being able to operate with a great deal of autonomy, until now.

True to her duty as Snake's 'moat dragon,' Melanie took a call from Snake's boss, Mr. Hardesty.

"Mr. Wormwood isn't available at the moment, I can take a message, sir," she said.

"Ms. Murphy, please don't take this wrong. I know you're only doing your job but I don't care where he is or what he is doing. I want him here in my office as soon as humanly possible. I take it I'm making myself clear," Hardesty said with as much reserve as he could muster.

"Yes, sir, I'll make sure he receives your instructions right away. Will that be all?"

"Yes, Ms. Murphy, that will be all."

Melanie Murphy heard the click on the other end and the line went dead. Wormwood hadn't come out of his office since he arrived early in the morning. There hadn't been any other incoming calls, so she wondered just what he was doing in there with the door shut.

She knocked twice.

"Enter," Wormwood responded in a weary voice.

"Mr. Wormwood, that was Mr. Hardesty on the phone. He said…"

"I know, I know," Wormwood interrupted, then rose to his feet and grabbed his overcoat. "I don't know if I'll be coming back, Mel. Thanks for everything."

He stepped past her and headed out.

"…that he wanted you to report to his office immediately," she said, completing the delivery the message from Hardesty.

Snake burned through eight minutes navigating his way across town and over to Langley. It took another five to park and go through security. He still had his coat on when he stood in front of Hardesty's desk. His boss had his chair swiveled in the opposite direction to emphasize the gravity of the exchange that was about to take place.

Snake was speechless when Hardesty finally swung around to face him. Snake could feel Hardesty's eyes boring into him even before the older man spoke a word.

"Mr. Randolph 'Sss-naye-eke' Wormwood," Hardesty said to him with a hiss, expressing distaste for Wormwood's nickname, as well as for his operating style. "Let me lay some facts on the table and we'll see what you have to say about where we go from here."

Snake had some idea about what his boss was obligated to remind him of, but hadn't a clue what was going to happen next.

"We took great pains, a great deal of time and resources, to say nothing of the lives spent on this operation so far," he began. "We lose contact with the source in Iran, then our backup plan fails because we couldn't keep your old buddy Coolhand in custody. God knows where he is now, and with what he knows, I don't even want to think about the consequences. And now, Christ, now we have a problem that has gotten completely out of hand. They even have a name for it now. Did you know? Do you even have any idea how dirty this whole thing has gotten? That damn drone we sent over there makes us look even more stupid."

Hardesty took a breath and tried to calm himself. He saw that he struck a nerve with Wormwood when the UAV was mentioned.

"Maybe that drone was just enough eye wash to keep the Iranians wondering just what the fuck happened to their precious project, but I doubt it. Now, we need to pull a hat trick, or both of us are going down. Any ideas?"

Hardesty looked over at Snake still standing three feet in front of his desk, wearing his overcoat and still red-faced from the cold. "Go ahead and take your coat off and pull up a chair, Snake. Consider yourself thoroughly chewed out."

Hardesty reached down and slid open the bottom drawer of his desk and pulled out a bottle of Chivas Regal and a pair of cut crystal tumblers. He poured two fingers into each glass and leaned forward to hand one of them to Snake.

"It seemed like things were going well there at first," said Hardesty.

"At least their enrichment progress has been halted for a while longer," Snake added.

"But they aren't stymied in the least. We failed in our main objective and next time it is going to be even more difficult, if not impossible to keep them from succeeding."

"Sir, you said there is a name on this mess already?"

"Yes. STUXNET. I don't even know what that means or who coined it, but damn it, somehow that thing that your boys put together didn't stay contained in the presumably closed network at the facility in Iran."

"What? Impossible!" Snake sounded incredulous. "It got loose?"

"Yes. Like the worst kind of germ warfare scenario during the cold war era. Ever wonder why we never used any of those tactics?"

Snake knew not to answer with a statement of the obvious. "Where? Who?"

"Friends, allies, the Germans, to be precise. The good news is that the malware your boys came up with can only infect systems networked in conjunction with server units built by Siemens."

"Sir, that was the intent. So, knowledge of this computer virus isn't out there on the internet working into every Tom, Dick, and Harry system?"

"We're not sure. As soon as the team in Germany detected the presence of malware knocking at the door, they were able to quickly divert the problem from infecting any of their systems. Thank God for our tight coordination. They alerted NSA right away. Now, we have all the best and brightest from the Symantec folks all the way to an underground group of hackers we're currently paying obscene amounts of money for, putting a lid on what we think was the entry path."

"Who, what, or where do they think that might be?"

"A physical fitness website. One of those sites where athletes enter their training data so that they can get ripped off by some health food supplement manufacturer or something like that. Anyway, that was the entry door. Our team and the folks in Israel have managed to contain things for now, but we've got egg all over our faces.

There's still no reaction from the Iranians. They obviously know something but aren't letting on. We're completely cut off from them at the moment. Our sources in Tehran are going quiet. Too dangerous to make contact with them. You made sure the others will likely remain silent when you took out that guy Heydar, or whatever his name was. Good move, by the way. I think your instincts were correct. The timing was all off, though, and who could have anticipated our key source would be a fitness fanatic."

Snake just sat sipping the Chivas from the glass his boss gave him. He didn't have anything to add while taking in all these latest bits of facts. *STUXNET*, he thought. It always amazed him how quickly people seem to want labels attached to everything. Almost as if it were planned ahead of time. However, he knew that with the operation in Iran, that wasn't the case.

"I need a plan. Any plan by 0800 tomorrow morning," Hardesty told Snake. "That's when I brief the President. Anything that gives us plausible deniability will work. Anything."

Hardesty set his empty glass on the desk and got up from his chair, signaling to Snake that it was time for him to gather his coat and get to work. Before closing the door to Hardesty's office on his way out, Snake told his boss, "Sir, we'll find Coolhand. We had a lead on him but the trail ran dry. His last known location was a bus depot in Baltimore. It won't be long. We've also got NSA working on this with us."

Snake drove back to his office, grateful his boss didn't ask for more details about what happened after they lost Reynolds at the bus depot. When the local Sheriff handed over the laptop to one of Snake's field officers, Snake learned it had been recovered by a bum on the bus. He realized Reynolds was going to be difficult to apprehend. He also knew finding him was the only clear option available to him.

CHAPTER 23

8 December 2011 - IBIR NEWS - Tehran, Iran

Reza's attention was glued to the media, the TV, Radio, and printed news. First, there were the images taken from strategic positions around the Natanz facility at ground level. The photos were the same ones that were published in the glossy media magazines. The next set of images was a group of stock photos of a stealth UAV used by American forces and said to be photographed while taking off from an airbase in Afghanistan. Finally, the images of soldiers in Iranian military uniforms holding pieces of the destroyed aircraft near a crash site in the vicinity of Natanz.

The images lead into the headline story that played in Tehran and the rest of the world. Like many Iranians, Reza knew that without diplomatic ties to the United States and the U.N. Security Council, The Islamic Republic of Iran's President, Mahmoud

Ahmadinejad, had few avenues available to him for engaging in strategic negotiation.

The latest news did nothing to stifle Reza's fear of what might happen to him if the authorities found out about his role in the destruction of the nuclear facility. Reza watched the screen as the Iranian President stood before the TV Camera with the flag of the republic in the background, declaring that the vicious attacks on his country's peaceful nuclear energy program were unjustified.

"The people of Iran will not stand for imperialist intervention in our peaceful development of vital energy sources," he said. "Our experts from the Ministry of Intelligence and National Security of the Islamic Republic of Iran have uncovered evidence that a collaboration existed between the United States and the illegitimate state of Israel that caused the interference at one of our facilities in Natanz. Iranians have every right to clean energy."

Reza hadn't been getting any sleep. Days earlier, he tried to warn his wife, Termeh, that there were government officials asking lots of questions about his work.

"If you are so scared, Farrokh, you should leave this job and we can return to Tehran. We can stay with my parents and you can maybe teach at the university instead of getting yourself tangled in this madness," she offered.

"I don't think you understand how serious things have become," he added. "I'm worried for your safety above all else."

"I can take care of myself and have been for quite some time. You need not worry about me. My professional connections will ensure my safety. Our government needs trained medical professionals and I've proven myself an asset to them," she rationalized.

"I think we should leave Termeh."

"Leave? And go where, Farrokh. Tell me, what do you know of living outside of Iran?"

"I have a friend who used to visit Cyprus. He showed me pictures. It is a beautiful and peaceful place. Wait just a minute and I'll show you."

Reza went into the den that he and his wife shared as a study. Most of the things in the room were Termeh's, since Reza did most of his work at his office in Isfahan. He sifted through a few pamphlets and books on one of the shelves where he kept his mementos from the various running events he'd competed in. Resting next to a small, framed photograph of him standing next to his running partner, Heydar, was the postcard Reza wanted to show his wife.

"See, it is sunny and you can almost tell from the pictures on the front that it is a quiet and peaceful place. We could go there for a while. Just until things here settle down," he said.

Termeh looked at the photo images on the front of the post card. She flipped the card over and noted the handwritten note from her husband's friend.

Reza - The 15 km run I took along the waterfront this morning was wonderful but toward the end, very hot. I hope your training continues well for you. See you next week - Heydar

Still holding the postcard, Termeh noted the printed location of the pictures on the front. It said, "Amathus Hotel and Beach Resort - Limassol Cyprus."

"A vacation would be wonderful, but we'd never be allowed to leave. Not now, with all this hype in the media. It would be different if you weren't somehow connected," she said, handing the postcard back to him.

"I suppose you're right," he said, and dropped the subject altogether.

The conversation he had with Termeh about the trip to Cyprus seemed like a fading memory. Now, seeing the news broadcast, Reza was becoming even more frightened. He was the one and only person who could have opened the doorway for the STUXNET virus to infect the network that hosted the command and control for the centrifuges. If the official investigators found out, he knew he'd be imprisoned for the rest of his life.

He continued watching the IBIR newscast. His country's president declared that officials had evidence of the cyber-attack that came from either the United States or Israel. How the president knew this was a mystery, but what he said next was real cause for concern.

"The Islamic Republic is a 'Nuclear Power.' Through the development of our peaceful energy program, our scientists and engineers have enriched enough uranium and weapons-grade material to be included among the selfish nations who tried to keep us out of the exclusive club of those possessing this power.

The intentions of the Islamic Republic of Iran's nuclear program has always been peaceful…until recently. The people of Iran ask those responsible for the destruction of our investment in the peaceful energy program in our country to come forward. We already know who you are. Mr. Barak Obama, your 'Olympic Games' operation was a failure. And you, Mr. Benjamin Netanyahu, cannot hide.

The Army of the Guardians of the Islamic Republic has established a target at an undisclosed location that only a select few in my country are aware of. It is a high-profile location that if destroyed, would cause more than just physical harm, but a new world order for others to consider. What we ask is the following:

The Islamic Republic of Iran requests an apology and cooperation from the culprit or culprits of the attack on our country. What has already happened is an act of war and it is by the peaceful graces of the Iranian people that there have not yet been reprisals. We have not had diplomatic relations with the United States or their puppet colony in the Levant for many years.

This is your chance to re-open the door to diplomacy and accept responsibility for the consequences of past actions. You have until the seventeenth of January to make your formal plea. Anticipating the question as to the date, the seventeenth was the date President Bush Senior of the United States started all of this for the Islamic people. We want you to remember your DESERT STORM, and your imperialist tinkering in matters you'll never understand."

Upon hearing the latest news, Reza went into a high state of anxiety and knew his only chance at a future would be to leave Iran immediately. The big question was how would he proceed and where would he go.

CHAPTER 24

11 December 2011 - Port of Baltimore, Maryland

Mark wished he'd been able to leave sooner, but it took an extra three days of moving from one cheap hotel to another before he obtained what he needed from the crypto-anarchist he found on Craigslist.

Coolhand never met or made contact with the person or the organization that produced a Canadian Passport complete with his alias printed inside, a photograph of him wearing heavy, plastic-rimmed glasses, and the latest RFID technology used by Canadian and U.S. Immigration imbedded in the back flap. He purchased both the passport photo and reading glasses with cash from a Rite Aid pharmacy near the waterfront.

The document transaction was done via dead drop at a dog park. Mark left one of his Green Dot Debit cards with $500 on it inside a green container used to dispense courtesy poop bags for the dog owners who might have forgotten to bring their own. In the early morning hours, he placed it in one of the doggie bags and stuffed it all the way into the bottom of the dispenser.

Mark didn't even know the name of the person or what they would look like. He was told to return as soon as possible after mid-day and his package would be waiting, similarly wrapped in one of the green doggy poop bags placed in the bottom of the dispenser.

His new Canadian passport had an authentic number and matching name that the clandestine distributor guaranteed was tested on a U.S. Customs and Border Protection RFID scan. Mark was confident he'd have no difficulty leaving the United States with it. However, he wasn't willing to take the chance of getting picked up at an airport. The latest news coming out of Iran had Homeland Security at its highest level of alert since 9/11.

Mark found the news disturbing because he knew the Iranians weren't kidding around. Picking off one of our stealth drones was justified, given that flying it into their sovereign airspace could be considered an act of war. Ahmadinejad took the upper hand and applied it with force by threatening to detonate a weapon. The question was not when, but where. Ahmadinejad clearly laid out a timetable for the culprits to come forward. Iran's actual readiness to follow through with their threat was still a question, but Mark knew it wasn't something to be tested.

Mark knew that by retracing his steps back to the Levant region of the Mediterranean, he'd get closer to learning who might have been involved in the scheme that held the U.S. and Israel at risk.

While waiting for his passport, Mark took notice of the commercial shipping traffic scheduled in and out of the Port of Baltimore. He found out that freighters and their crews based in the United States were bonded. The crews were all part of a longshoreman's union, making it nearly impossible to seek passage in exchange for shipboard labor. This was not the case with foreign shipping.

The converted Russian Freighter, *"Yuyri Ostrovskiy"* was scheduled to leave in the late evening with the outgoing tide. The ship was perfect for Mark's purpose. It was a rust bucket that looked like it had seen better days, but seaworthy and large enough that the passage wouldn't be too uncomfortable. Best of all, though, the ship was bound for Sevastopol on the Black Sea, with Bizerte, Tunisia and Limassol, Cyprus as ports of call enroute.

His first inclination was to stow away, but he dismissed the idea because of the problems of provisions and comfort. Instead, he figured he'd simply buy off the captain. Track him down, meet him in a bar, fill him with a few drinks and offer cash for passage. That is exactly what he did two days later.

"Vasilli Gurovich?" Mark asked the man sitting in a darkened bar tucked away in the industrial neighborhood near the commercial shipping port. "Captain of the *Yuyri Ostrovskiy?*"

"Who asks? I don't owe anybody money. In fact, I don't owe anybody anything," said the wrinkled, overweight Russian sporting at least a two-day growth of grey whiskers.

Mark could smell the vodka on the sea captain's breath. "Buy you another?" he offered.

"I don't like Americans. Never have," the Russian said, not acknowledging Mark's offer.

"I'm Canadian," Mark told him. "The name's Allen Cole."

"In that case, yes, another vodka. What brings you to this stinking hole Mr. Canadian, what was your name again? Yes, Mr. Cole."

"Allen. Just call me Allen," Mark said, and signaled the bar tender for two more drinks. "I was thinking of doing some business with you. That is, if you are interested."

"I don't do private deals. I have a merchant mariner's license that has been my ticket to this wonderful life," he spread both his arms to show Mark that drinking in the wharf side bar was a sort of penultimate experience. "Why would I risk my license for a Canadian who wants to use me to smuggle something for him?" the captain asked, still probing for the possibility of a business transaction.

"Just a ride and a place to sleep. That's all I'm looking for.

Nothing illegal. You won't have to worry about losing your license," Mark assured him.

"No girls or young boys. I don't transport people. My cousin, Vlad, is still in a Ukrainian jail because authorities found a container converted into a travel pod for human trafficking. This trading in human commodity is a terrible thing. I have my principles. Serves Vlad right. I hope he rots in jail." The Russian knocked back the remains of his vodka and set the glass down on the bar.

Mark pulled out a large roll of bills wrapped in a rubber band and set it on the bar in front of Vasilli. "There's $2500, cash. I've got another roll just like it that I can give you when we cast off. Go on, take it, I'll be by tomorrow afternoon and you can decide whether we have a deal."

"How many people?" asked the captain, looking over at Mark from under his brow.

"Just me. I'm the traveler."

"What did you do, kill your wife?" the captain laughed, then coughed as he asked his rhetorical question.

Mark looked at him and laughed also. "No, I'm a journalist. I'm doing a freelance piece about the lost art of tramping."

"My ship is not a tramp and don't ever let me catch you or anyone referring to her as anything other than the most efficient freighter in her class. She's got three 110,000 horse power

Wartsilla turbo diesels and can make the passage to Bizerte in under six days. You say good things about the *Yuyri Ostrovskiy*, okay, then you can sit at my table for breakfast."

"So, we have a deal then?"

"Yes, a deal. You don't need to come down here tomorrow. Just show up with your sea bag and tell the purser on the gangplank that Vasilli wants you escorted to the bridge. That way, you can pay me the rest of the charge for passage when we, what did you call it? 'Cast off,' the captain said, giving Mark a disapproving expression.

CHAPTER 25

24 December 2011 - Somewhere near Salmas Kurdistan

Reza had been on the run for just under a week. Knowing he would eventually be singled out for having planted STUXNET in the closed network at Natanz, he gathered his backpacking and hiking gear and left Isfahan on a train. Reza had no other option. He was scared and knew that he'd have to travel over land in order to get out of Iran.

He elected to take a train to Tabriz in the north where he hopped on an overcrowded bus that took him into Kurdish country west of Salmas. There, the road was just a dirt track that ended in a high, mountainous area with a series of trails leading further west into Turkey and Iraq.

Reza thought how nice it would have been to take an adventure vacation in these mountains just to hike and camp as he did with his uncle when he was a teenager. Instead, he was driving himself to exhaustion in order to be weary enough to escape his fears, just so he could attain an uncomfortable slumber each night.

When Reza had figured out that the wrist watch Heydar gave him was the likely culprit, he had smashed it into the ground and took the pieces into the basement of his office complex in Isfahan. He burned the evidence in the boiler room.

He figured it would have only been a matter of time before the officials picked him up for another interrogation. Without Heydar in the picture, he knew he'd become the one who would take a public blame and be labeled an imperialist spy. In his line of thinking, what could be the risk of escaping Iran through Kurdistan?

So, there he was, trudging through snow on his way to Turkey with only one clue to guide him. His only lead was to find a man named Marios who frequented the Amathus Hotel Resort in Limassol Cyprus.

Before Reza had left Isfahan, he'd stopped at the university's gym locker room to collect his winter running gear he had stored in his locker. He wasn't sure what sparked his curiosity, but he acted on it anyway. Before leaving with his gym duffle, he attempted to pick the lock of Heydar's locker. Reza had no experience with such things and quickly gave up. Instead, he pried the locker's flimsy door open with the imitation Swiss Army Knife Termeh gave him for his birthday several years ago.

There wasn't much in Heydar's locker. He found a pair of racing flats that had hardly been worn. He recognized them, having seen his running partner wearing them during one of their track workouts for the first time a couple of months earlier. Reflecting back, it seemed like a lifetime ago.

"Nice shoes," Reza commented to his friend when they met on the track.

"Yes, these need to be properly broken in," said Heydar.

"You can't get the racing Asics here in Iran. Where did you pick them up?"

"My last trip to Cyprus. These days you can buy almost anything there. The Russians have made sure of it," Heydar replied.

"Black Market? You didn't really buy them off a black market did you?" Reza asked.

"I wouldn't know for sure. All I know is that these are some comfortable shoes and I intend to wear them for the marathon we will run together in November."

Reza jolted himself from the memory of that workout when he reached further into Heydar's locker and found a nylon gym duffle. He slid it toward himself and a zippered sweatshirt spilled from the bag along with a book of matches.

Reza bent down to pick up the matchbook. He noticed the glossy, blue-colored photo on the front. It was a picture of a beachfront Hotel. Reza recognized it immediately as the same one on the post card he'd received from Heydar. It said, "Amathus Hotel, CY."

When he opened the matchbook, there weren't any missing matches. On the inside flap was a name written in blue ink. The block letters read, "Marios" 1437 Pano Platres. It was an address and Reza made his decision at that very moment to go there and find the man, Marios.

After slogging through the snows of eastern Turkey and getting a ride or traveling by bus whenever he could, Reza became more and more obsessed with the idea of the Amathus Hotel on a warm sunny beach.

The difficult part of his escape from Iran was nearing an end when he reached the Turkish coast at a village named Mersin on the Mediterranean. Reza found a fisherman that agreed to drop him near Lachi Cyprus.

The fisherman warned Reza that even though he could drop him off at Kyrenia, traveling through Nicosia to the South on an Iranian passport could be problematic.

Reza took the hint and paid the fisherman handsomely for delivering him to southern Cyprus without any bureaucratic hiccups. From Lachi, he would easily find a bus heading for Limassol.

CHAPTER 26

5 January 2012 - Haifa, Israel

Mark would have enjoyed the trip over the Atlantic and through the Straites of Gibraltar, had he been on a pleasure cruise. Even though the passage wasn't cheap for Mark, the idea had a certain romantic quality.

He'd only been to Cyprus once while performing his attaché duties for the Ambassador in Tel Aviv. He was confident he wouldn't have any trouble getting around. From Limassol, his plan was to return to Tel Aviv via fast ferry where he'd begin his search for the woman named Rina. During his crossing of the Mediterranean, Mark had plenty of time to think, so he replayed each and every day he could remember from his time in Israel. Recalling intelligence reports and the various interactions with the CIA Station Chief during the Ambassador's weekly country update, Mark remembered one very critical piece of information that would prove helpful in his quest.

It was about three weeks prior to his meeting with Jessup, the same day as their regular tennis match and the bistro dinner that ended in a bloody disaster, his last memory of Israel. CIA Station Chief Smith had some questions regarding Israel's drone programs and requested that Mark join him in his office following the weekly country meeting. The meeting wasn't the least bit remarkable. Smith's questions were straightforward and Mark was anxious to collaborate as much as possible, never knowing when the favor might be reciprocated.

What he saw was not totally out of place. It confirmed that he was, indeed, immersed in the center of an operating environment where things aren't always what they seem on the surface. On the low counter below the wooden bookcase in Smith's office were several framed photographs. In one of them was a group of women seated on a balcony overlooking a crowded street. In the photograph were people marching with purple and rainbow-colored signs. There were men wearing pink boas and women with shaven heads wearing nothing but black leather vests.

When Smith noticed Mark studying the photo, he commented, "That was taken at the Gay Pride Parade in Beer Sheba last summer. It caused quite a stir within the Israeli government."

Mark just nodded. He wasn't at all curious about the parade. His attention was drawn to the blonde woman dressed in conservative summer clothing, not like what she wore when he first met her in the company of his tennis opponent Colonel Jessup.

"Who are these people seated on the balcony in this picture?" Mark asked.

"Interesting you should ask," Smith replied. "The woman on the far left is the wife of the Canadian Cultural Attaché. Her name is Penny Cranston. Seated next to her is a woman named Rina Cohen, at least that is the name she uses. To Ms. Cohen's right is the girlfriend of the Ambassador's oldest son, we don't know much about her family, but the young lady is only about nineteen years old. We've had the good fortune of benefiting from the relationship between the Canadian woman and one of my guys. Ms. Penny Cranston apparently doesn't get enough from her husband. As for my guy? Well, let's just say he could get by moonlighting at Chip and Dale's. As you might imagine, these connections enable us to keep tabs on the boss's son."

Mark got the sense that Smith enjoyed his work and the opportunity to roll around in other people's dirt. "This woman, Rina Cohen, what's her story?" Coolhand asked of the station chief, knowing there was more to it.

"We suspect she's Mossad. No, I take that back, she's probably Mossad, but we have no way of confirming it. Do you recognize her from somewhere?" Smith asked.

"We may have crossed paths a few months ago is all."

"Casual or involved?" asked Smith.

"Definitely casual. On the arm of one of my Israeli counterparts."

"Jessup?"

"I won't even ask how you knew that but, yes."

A fresh, salty breeze brought Mark back into the present as he stood on the deck of the tourist ferry that would transport him from Limassol to Haifa, Israel. Mark was intent on his mission to locate Rina Cohen. He envisioned that, together, they could find out the origins of STUXNET and turn the information over to international authorities, stopping the Iranian leadership from inflicting any harm or crime against humanity as Ahmadinejad had previously threatened.

CHAPTER 27

6 January 2012 - Limassol, Cyprus

When Reza arrived in Limassol via bus, it was late afternoon. He was weary from the travel and everything that transpired over the past months. Only weeks ago when he was snow shoeing through the passes of eastern Turkey, he promised himself that when he made it to Limassol he would check into the Amathus Hotel, order room service and soak in a hot bath.

Though Cyprus is known to be a warm, sunny vacation spot for Europeans, in January it can be cool, dark and rainy. Reza was pleased to discover that the off-season made everything less expensive. Though he was burning through his savings, he knew his life in Iran was finished. He could never go back. Reza began to realize he was on a one-way mission to prevent World War Three.

The next morning, Reza awoke refreshed from his travels and

tribulations. He knew his mission depended upon his successful contact with the man Marios, who presumably lived in a village named Pano Platres. From the hotel concierge, Reza obtained a reservation for a rental car and asked about the village that he only knew by name.

By mid-day, Reza was in a rented car, driving on a winding road in the foothills of the Troodos. Pano Platres was a small village served by a narrow, one-way road that looped back and forth up a terraced landscape. There were two or three family-owned patio restaurants that were obviously closed for the season. The only sign of life was a coffee house that had its lights on. A couple of older men sat on wooden chairs watching a television mounted on a wall in the far corner.

Reza couldn't find anything resembling an address and he'd already driven two laps of the only road cutting through the village, so he stopped in at the coffee house to ask for directions. The older men watching the television eyed him when he entered. Reza nodded a gesture of hello but the men just stared.

In back of the coffee counter, a man emerged from behind a curtain covering a doorway leading to a store room. The man said something to Reza in Greek, which Reza didn't respond to.

"I'm sorry, I thought you spoke Greek," said the proprietor.

"I was hoping to find someone who could help me with locating an address," said Reza with a smile for the proprietor.

LAMB

"Sure, I've lived here my whole life. Where are you trying to go?"

"The only address I have is One-Four-Three-Seven, Pano Platres."

"You are standing in the middle of Pano Platres at this very moment. One-Four-Three-Seven does not sound like a familiar number. We haven't used address numbers for our village homes since I was a boy. I think, though, that it is good. There is a postal delivery that probably uses it."

"How do I find out if the postal service uses this address number?"

"There is a postal service office in Kakopatria, just the other side of the mountain. It is probably closer than driving all the way back to Limassol, which is where our village mail comes from," said the proprietor.

It took twenty minutes for Reza to reach Kakopatria and locate the post service office, which was nothing more than a rundown, brick building next to a larger space that was used as some kind of granary or warehouse. The directions he got from the postal clerk took him to a long, shaded lane just northeast of the small village center in Pano Platres where he was earlier.

At the end of the lane, the drive circled around a fountain in front of a large building mostly hidden from view. The building was much bigger than almost the entire village of Pano Platres. It was the "Forest Park Hotel."

Reza didn't go to the reception desk when he arrived. Instead, he climbed a flight of stairs to the first floor and took a turn down a long hall, where at the end of it, he found the door to a luxury suite. The number on the door was One-Four-Three-Seven. Reza didn't care that it didn't make sense to have discovered the address on a matchbook from a hotel with a different name. He figured perhaps Heydar met the man Marios at the Amathus Hotel before Marios gave him the address where he lived.

After knocking several times, Reza heard the sounds of movement coming from behind the door with the number One-Four-Three-Seven emblazoned on the heavy, dark wood.

Then, came the grumpy voice of a man complaining in Greek as he opened the door to his guest.

"I'm sorry to bother you," said Reza in heavily accented English.

The tall, dark-haired, olive-skinned man staring back at Reza had bloodshot eyes and smelled of alcohol. He was wearing tan slacks, and an oversized white tee shirt. "Come in. Please, sit," Marios said in perfect English.

The suite was well-appointed. It looked as though the man actually lived in the hotel room. There were personal belongings on every shelf. Had Reza known the means by which this man made his living, he would have been surprised at the invitation to come inside.

"I was actually expecting someone else, but if you've come to kill me, I suggest you do it quickly. I'm in no mood for any charades," Marios said.

Reza lifted his empty hands to Marios, swiveling his head from side to side and said, "No, you misunderstand. My best friend and running partner, Heydar, went missing in Iran. I'm looking for him,"

Reza thought this man Marios must have recognized his accent because he shot back in Farsi, "You are a nuclear engineer."

At first, Reza was shocked, and then as the two men continued their conversation, he became more relaxed.

"You weren't my first visitor in these past months. You see, nothing out of the ordinary goes unnoticed here in Cyprus, but this is the first I've heard of the loss of your friend. I'm very sorry" Marios said. "If you'll forgive me, I must seem out of sorts to you."

Reza didn't know what to say, so he remained silent, waiting for Marios to continue.

"As you may have guessed, I was anticipating someone else. Things for me have turned for the worst and I resigned myself to the knowledge that someone who's set on killing me will eventually succeed," Marios said before the two men pieced together the events that resulted in their present meeting in the Troodos.

"I probably shouldn't ask, but how does one become so entangled in such a complicated web?" Reza asked.

The two men continued their conversation. Reza was intrigued by Marios's background. He discovered Marios was a man without a country.

"I was at one time an Iranian citizen," Marios told him. "I'd been supplying the Syrian government with sensitive information while working out of Beirut before the Marine barracks were bombed in the Fall of eighty-three. None of us had any place to go. It was a cold war and I was in the only business that I knew. My contact in Syria still owed me. He set me up with an American with deep pockets and some reliable pay. That is why I was rewarded with this untenable situation."

Reza thought Marios probably shared more than he should have. It didn't matter, Reza wanted Marios to tell him more about how he forged a life in Cyprus without a national citizenship. He was hoping the man Marios could guide him to a better future.

CHAPTER 28

6 January 2012 - Tel Aviv, Israel

Mark was looking for Rina Cohen. He figured she'd be laying low after the botched mission. He imagined she must have been still reeling from the events that caused Jessup's death. Now, with the operation finished, he was seeking answers. She was the only one he knew to confront that might have knowledge of using the secret designer drug that, weeks earlier, took him out of the picture.

Mark's search for information was riding on a very thin thread. The name Rina Cohen was all he had to go on, as were his recollections from their first encounter over a year ago. Back then, she told him over dinner that she curated at an art studio near Hayarkon Park, in the northern district of Tel Aviv. "Blue" was the name of the place, she told him. Rather, the actual name she gave him for the gallery was "Tekehelet," but after her explanation of the word, he remembered it simply as "Blue."

Mark was familiar with that section of town, so after he checked into the familiar Holiday Inn on the beachfront, he followed the instructions the concierge gave him and located Heimie's Haberdashery, where he paid cash to be outfitted in some stylish clothing. He needed to fit in with the rest of the street traffic in Tel Aviv's wealthiest district.

For a ghost who'd just spent the better part of a couple of weeks at sea, Mark thought he looked the part of a wealthy Israeli as he walked up the main sidewalk opposite the row of galleries where he hoped to find Tekehelet.

He used the reflection from the shop window to check for any sign of being followed. While he made himself appear to be looking into the window, he focused his attention on the reflection of the shop across the street. The lighting inside of Tekehelet made it possible for him to see the people inside. There was an older couple inspecting a glass sculpture on a pedestal in the main display area. After a few minutes, Mark saw the blonde woman. Rina Cohen looked almost as she did when Jessup introduced them many months ago, only she was more conservatively dressed.

The couple looking at the art was just browsing and left when Ms. Cohen came over to assist them. When the couple made their exit from Tekehelet, Mark took his cue and walked another fifty feet before crossing the road two doors down from Tekehelet's entrance. No other patrons came or left the gallery since the older couple's departure.

When Mark entered, Rina Cohen was in the far corner repositioning something behind a small counter. She looked up as he approached and didn't recognize him at first. Then, suddenly she locked onto his eyes and made a quick turn for the back hall only a few feet away.

"Oh, no you don't, young lady," said Mark in a tone elevated by adrenalin.

Cohen took one look at Mark and feared for her life. She thought he'd been sent back to Israel by the people she'd been working for, perhaps to clean up some tracks in the wake of the car bombing that killed one of her colleagues.

She dashed down the hall with Mark just an arm's length away. He thought she couldn't be armed or she'd have pulled a weapon on him by now. Without a weapon himself, he was taking a big chance. Furthermore, he knew if this woman wanted to, she could make it a difficult round of hand to hand combat for him.

"Please, Ms. Cohen. We're on the same side in this. I know who you are. MIDVIEW!" he shouted at her. "Does that ring any bells, or would it sound better to your ear if I said the whole thing, MIDVIEW-ULTRA?"

The woman stopped in her tracks. Her right hand was still clutching at the door lever. When she turned to look at Mark there were tears streaming from her eyes. Rina Cohen knew she couldn't hide. Not from Mark and not from the Mossad. She was instructed to lay low after the car bombing and was told to await further instructions from a contact who worked for a defense industry partner.

"Let's go someplace where we can talk," Mark said.

Although the woman was a well-trained Mossad operative, she gave off the impression that the fight had gone out of her. Attacking Mark at this point would have drawn undue attention, possibly creating a bigger problem for her later. She thought by cooperating, she'd have a better chance to learn why he'd returned to Tel Aviv.

Mark escorted Rina Cohen away from the gallery and toward Hayarkon Park. They walked together, side by side, as if they were a couple stewing on a domestic dispute in need of resolution. Mark led Rina over to a concrete bench where the two of them sat beneath an olive tree.

"I'm dead," Mark told her.

"So am I," the woman told him.

"No, I mean, there must have been some reason to keep me alive. The media reported my death in that car bomb explosion that killed Jessup in Haifa. I need you to help me unravel a few things."

"I don't know what you're talking about," she said.

"Yes, you do. You know something about administering hallucinogenic drugs to unsuspecting human intelligence operatives. I'm pretty sure you know what I'm talking about," he said.

"Okay, yes. I've heard of MV-ULTRA. It isn't something that is deployed very often," she confessed.

"Rina, listen, there was an operation in Iran last month."

"I know. I watch the news. Shouldn't you be back in the United States? Someplace safer than right here at ground zero? I hear the Iranians have already placed a device someplace in our country. It is only a matter of time before millions of people die."

"You sure sound like a fatalist. Hear me out, there is a connection and you're my only lead. We can stop bad things from happening if you would just reason with me for a moment."

"Okay, I'm ready to reason. How can we possibly change the inevitable?"

"Somehow, that malware virus got into Iran's nuclear facility. After the facility was destroyed, and the US drone was shot down, there was car bombing here, in Israel. Those events all seem to coincide. I don't buy the coincidence. Someone is behind all this and we're going to go through all the names and connections of those still alive until we can piece together a common thread."

Mark sensed Rina Cohen was allowing her armor and defensive barriers to come down and he listened while she told him everything she knew. "How do you know about MIDVIEW-ULTRA?" She asked.

Mark laughed. Not loud, but to her face and wagged his head back and forth, "Really? You have to ask?"

"Yes, it is important, I think."

"I was a target. I got to experience the effects of that weapon firsthand and still can't figure out how or when I could have been exposed." Then, Mark went on to tell Rina what he remembered about his experience from the time he and Jessup drove back from Caesarea after playing tennis. When he was finished, he asked her, "You had some part in MIDVIEW-ULTRA, didn't you?"

For a moment, Rina just stared at him, appearing to be completely at a loss for words. Then, everything came flooding out. "There were two of us trained in the various ways to infect the target with a dose of the drug," she said. "We were both told exactly when and to whom it would be administered. I had no idea what the long-term effect would be, but was told it was designed to render the target useless, but not immobile. The target would be unable to remember anything for approximately thirty-six hours."

"Who was the other agent who you trained with?" Mark asked her.

"She's dead. She was with Jessup when the car bomb exploded."

Mark understood immediately that Rina had been trained for a one-way mission, which explained why she had no trouble telling him everything.

"What did you know about the other coincidences that I mentioned? The drone and the centrifuges at Natanz?" he asked.

"I'm not familiar with anything having to do with drones. Not unless you think the few evenings I spent with Jessup enjoying fancy dinners and cocktail gatherings with aerospace people mean anything. My controller would give me names of people to watch and report on. I documented who they spent time talking to, that is all. Why? I never found out. That is how we were trained to do our work," she told him.

"What about the other? Natanz?" Mark was really hoping she had something, but was afraid of the consequences if this trail was a dead end. They'd both probably get a chance to witness the wrath of some pissed off Iranians.

Mark listened while Rina continued. "There was one peculiar thing that comes to mind. I overheard Jessup on the phone a couple of times. He mentioned the name of someone named Marios. I wouldn't have thought much of it, but Marios was involved in another operation involving MID-VIEW back in 2007 on Cyprus," she told him.

"Let me guess, the Defense Attaché, Thomas Mooney, was somehow involved," said Mark.

"How would you know something like that?" she asked him.

"Tom was a colleague and the circumstances of his death didn't add up. So, this Marios had something to do with it?"

"We're getting off-track here, Colonel Reynolds. What happened to your colleague on Cyprus doesn't have anything to do with the centrifuges or drones."

"How do you know that? Maybe all of these things are somehow connected," insisted Mark.

"Ever since I heard Jessup utter his name, I've been digging around learning all I could find out about Marios. That is how I discovered his involvement in MIDVIEW-ULTRA. Then, after the car bomb exploded several weeks ago, I was called in.

I was instructed to return to the gallery and wait. That's what I've been doing ever since. Waiting for someone to come along and terminate me. Then, came the threats from the Iranians. I was thinking our people always seem to have their hands full, looking for a needle in a haystack, but when I was called in I heard them talking about Marios and the Iranian connection. None of it made sense," she said.

"Well, Ms. Cohen, something certainly makes sense to me," he declared. "Marios is our only hope of stopping the Iranians from doing something that will cause harm to millions of people. Any idea where to start looking for him besides combing the entire island of Cyprus to find him?"

Rina nodded and said, "Mossad is not good at recording

information about contacts and agents, but they are very good at honoring payment and for some reason, there was more detail in the accounting reports than I'd ever expected to see." She pulled out a slip of paper and wrote down the address in Pano Platres where Marios's payment for services was being sent.

Mark took the information from the Israeli woman, "Thank you. How about you coming with me? You look like you could benefit from getting away from all of this," he said.

"I wouldn't be getting away. I'd be running and when a Mossad operative runs, they are terminated. Good luck to you, Colonel," she said, and got up to walk back to the gallery, leaving Mark sitting on the bench alone.

CHAPTER 29

7 January 2012 - Arlington, Virginia

"He's been located?" Wormwood asked Jimmy while they both stood in the center of the basement operations center.

"Yes, sir. Reynolds was spotted making contact with a Mossad agent in the northern district of Tel Aviv early this morning," Jimmy replied.

"Are we keeping tabs on him? Someone is tailing him, I hope."

"No need, sir. We found out everything we needed from the woman."

"What woman?" asked Snake.

"The Mossad agent, sir."

"Mossad doesn't tell secrets. They'd rather die first," said Snake to nobody in particular. His small team of operatives missed a small detail. Rina Cohen was the sister of Rachel Jennings from the DIA. The psychologist was also the specialist in charge of every aspect of MIDVIEW-ULTRA. Jennings was in charge of running the female agents in Israel and other unnamed hot spots where American interests were at stake.

"Okay then, Jimmy, I'm ultimately responsible for the success of this next mission if that is what we'll be calling this clusterfuck we've been chasing around. Where the hell is Reynolds?"

Jimmy gave him the exact location where Marios could be found on Cyprus. "That Bitch!" said Snake. "How the fuck did she uncover him? Now, Reynolds will be going there and I've got to stop him. Stop both of them," he said.

"Sir, what about the Iranian threat?"

"Reynolds probably knows. We're going to fly by the seat of our pants on this one, Jimmy. If anyone asks where I am, you stay tight-lipped. Oh, and this bit of information you boys just uncovered, keep it to yourselves for the next thirty-six hours. I'll be in touch."

Snake left the ops room in a big hurry to figure out how he was going to beat Coolhand to Marios's location. Sure, he was interested in preventing a nuclear explosion provided courtesy of Mahmoud Ahmadinejad, but his burning desire came more from maintaining control of the situation and keeping his boss and those above him, all the way up to the President of the United States, happy.

CHAPTER 30

12 January 2012 - Pano Platres - Troodos, Cyprus

Before leaving Tel Aviv and returning to Cyprus, Mark had one more chore to accomplish. He met with Rina Cohen again the following morning, near the old harbor in Tel Aviv. As he'd anticipated, she arrived at the specified time with a small package she'd prepared.

"You remember the various ways this can be administered?" she asked him more as a reminder.

"Yes, I think I can figure it out," he replied.

"Your worst enemy when using this type of weapon is haste. Take your time and make sure you do a dry run before actually using it," she instructed.

"Is that what you and your colleagues did with me? Watched my actions? Conducted a practice run?" he asked, holding up the small, vinyl pouch Rina gave him and making a show of it for her.

LAMB

She didn't acknowledge his comment. "Just be careful. I hope you are successful in stopping all this madness."

"The timetable for the Iranian threat is pretty dramatic, the anniversary of DESERT STORM. Don't you think that is strange?" asked Mark.

"They believe they can only make their point with drama. Ahmadinejad is a very literal dictator and wants his moment in the sun. He's seeking respect. You must believe that we still have time to turn this situation back," she said, clasping both Mark's hands. "You will be successful. Then, you'll return to Israel and I'll buy you dinner."

Mark didn't know what to make of Rina's last statement. Maybe it was Rina's way of denying she'd made herself a marked woman. He knew it would only be a matter of time before Rina Cohen was detained and interrogated. How that might end was anybody's guess.

"Come to Cyprus with me. I know somebody who might be able to get you out of this," Mark said.

Rina shook her head. "You don't think there are people watching every move I make? My only hope is that you succeed."

"Rina, listen. Please. I know a way you can 'disappear,' just like I did.

"Mark. I appreciate the offer. Right now, we need to concentrate on the immediate problem. Once we take care of it, if

I'm still around, I promise I'll let you help me 'disappear.'"

The loose plan that Mark was piecing together, adapting to the changes in the tactical situation, involved identifying a likely scapegoat and working out a way to turn them over to Iranian officials. Mark figured that if the scapegoat he had in mind were credible enough, the Iranians would be pleased to learn how STUXNET was introduced into their facility.

For the Iranians to find out how the virus got into their system was a bargaining chip all by itself. What made the loose plan attractive to Mark was his choice of scapegoat. The person he had in mind knew just enough to keep the Iranians happy while serving as personal restitution for ruining his life. Mark's plan was to find a way to turn Randy "Snake" Wormwood over to MISIRI.

He figured he knew enough about Snake's lifestyle and habits that he'd be able to track him down in the bars of Arlington Virginia and hire some thugs to help detain him. But first, he had to find the man named Marios.

Mark had no idea what he'd find in room One-Four-Three-Seven of the "Forest Park Hotel" in the Troodos foothills of Mount Olympus on Cyprus. He had no way of knowing Snake was speeding across oceans and continents to beat him to their shared destination either.

This wasn't a situation where you just go up to the door and knock on it, he decided. Instead, after Mark parked his rental car in a spot behind the hotel where he would blend in with other off-season visitors, he decided to reconnoiter the place first, and find out if the man Marios was even staying in his suite.

Mark entered the hotel's main lobby and noticed the two clerks at the reception desk were busy checking out a large family dressed for skiing on Mt. Olympus. The hotel was large, given its location on the outskirts of the small village. Mark noticed the grounds were well-maintained as he proceeded through glass doors at the rear of the main lobby, where he stepped out into a sunlit courtyard.

He found what he'd hoped for under the eaves at the far end of the flagstone path leading to an archway and stairwell. He made his way over to the open archway. On the wall next to a fire extinguisher, he spotted the diagram outlining emergency escape routes for the occupants in case of a fire. Mark knew that all international hotels were required to post them in and around every exit, not just for the occupants, but for the rescuers as well.

With the emergency exit diagram, he studied the floor plan, thus locating room One-Four-Three-Seven. Once he was sure of its location, he took a tour of the courtyard and found an empty umbrella table where he sat down to think, blending in with the other guests.

A young Cypriot waiter dressed in black slacks and a white waistcoat came over to take Mark's order for a Cypriot coffee. A

Platres, the air warmed as the sun marched on a steady path above the horizon.

It was still early when he arrived at the Forest Hotel parking lot, so Snake decided he'd grab a catnap before staking out the suite where Marios was reported to be staying. Snake's car was one of the few in the parking area that was facing out. Earlier, he'd backed it into the stands of oleanders that ringed the lot. From his chosen position, he figured he'd be able to see anyone coming and going.

Mark was fortunate that Snake was slumped down in the driver's seat, deep in slumber from all the travel, when Mark pulled into the lot less than a half-hour later. Snake didn't notice Coolhand climbing the short flight of stairs to the main lobby. However, when the alarm he'd set on his watch awakened him an hour later, he resumed his surveillance of the lobby entrance and took note of each guest as they came or left.

***

Snake was hoping to see Coolhand coming to the hotel looking for Marios, but what happened next caused a drastic change in his plans. Two dark-haired men with olive-toned skin were leaving the hotel together. They were conversing as though they were friends. Even though Snake never met this man who'd been running dark ops for him, he knew the larger of the two men had to be Marios. When the taller, slightly overweight man and his skinny, shorter friend walked over to a convertible and removed the top to let the sun in for their drive, Snake reasoned that the other man had to have been his last connection to the Natanz operation.

Snake wouldn't accept the possibility of coincidence in this case, so he decided to follow Marios and his companion. He figured if Marios wasn't going to be at the hotel, then maybe he'd be wasting his time waiting for Coolhand. Regardless, he was going to find out what he could from this man, so he focused his attention on following them at a safe distance.

Mark watched in wonder at the scene unfolding before him. As the convertible drove away from the circuit in front of the hotel, Mark saw another vehicle depart from the far corner of the lot. Inside the white Astra with the window rolled down, was the unmistakable profile of none other than Randy " Snake" Wormwood.

Makes my job all the more easy, Mark thought. A convertible and a white rental on its tail, how hard could that be to track while traveling the vacant, off-season roads of Cyprus?

As the road widened on the northern outskirts of Limassol, Mark was still coming down the hill about a quarter-mile back. He closed the distance as the two vehicles in front of him entered a roundabout and turned south toward Limassol Harbor. He nearly lost them when a delivery truck pulled out of an alleyway perpendicular to the two-lane boulevard leading to the waterfront. He caught a glimpse of the convertible turning into a beachfront car park next to the small yacht basin. The small harbor was nestled near the west edge of town, adjacent to the commercial port.

As Mark caught up, he noted the white Astra making the turn into the same lot. Mark drove past with the intention of making a U-turn back around and parking on the street opposite. By the time he got out of his car, he could see Snake striding down the ramp leading to a network of docks and slips where both high-end and casual pleasure yachts were berthed.

Mark picked up the pace while trying not to move in a way that would draw anyone's attention. He wore a tennis cap he'd picked up at the hotel, figuring it, along with his wraparound sunglasses, would be enough to keep Snake from recognizing him at a distance. He also figured if he were carrying something, all the better.

He slipped the vinyl wallet with the MIDVIEW-ULTRA weapon into the travel duffle he brought with him from Tel Aviv. It was passable as a sailing duffle for a casual afternoon on Limassol Bay.

When Mark arrived at the top of the ramp, he saw Snake turning left beneath a sign that read L-Dock in both English and

Greek.

***

Earlier, while Reza and the man Marios were on their way to the small yacht harbor, they continued the conversation they'd started the evening before. Reza was happy to find Marios was in much better spirits since they met.

"As I said yesterday, I was feeling quite alone with my mission. It was hasty of our government to come up with such an ill-conceived plan," said Marios to his new friend, Reza. "We were both used by Ahmadinejad, but in different ways."

"But there was no reason for you to lose hope," said Reza, more for himself to believe than for Marios. "I still can't fathom how you were able to transport a nuclear device out of Iran without being detected."

"I had a lot of help. There was motivation on many sides. Ahmad's people didn't know what we were doing when they arranged for safe passage into Syria. My job was to sail to Latakia and have '*Scarlet*' hoisted out of the water for annual repairs."

"'*Scarlet?*'" Reza asked.

"Yes, she's a Nautor Swan 44. You will see her soon. Whatever MISIRI arranged with Ahmad's people to get the work done on her, I have no knowledge of besides the result. I returned to Tehran for a week and when I arrived back in Latakia four days ago, Scarlet was back in the water and ready to sail."

"So, the delivery method is the boat?" Reza asked.

"Yes. The lead keel was removed and replaced with the device sheathed in a thin layer of lead and incased in leak-proof carbon fiber. The weight of the device and lead sheathing was perfectly calculated to replace the ballast of the original keel. It also serves to shield the device from leaking radiation.

The detonator controls are routed to the navigation station in the main cabin. I'll show you when we get to the harbor. The passage from Latakia took only twenty hours. It would have been quicker had I left in the late morning when the winds were just starting to rage. By the time I set sail, though, it was a near gale and I had her reefed down to practically nothing. Then, two hours after sunset, the wind shut down entirely. It was a slog across using the auxiliary diesel engine for the rest of the trip."

"Were you supposed to sail to Haifa?" Reza asked.

"No. Not right away. So far, MISIRI believes I'm complying with orders. I was to await further instructions in Pano Platres."

"Well, they will certainly be disappointed when they try to reach you and you're not there."

"Serves them right. It would have been a one-way mission for me, but that wasn't why I got so drunk the night before you found me."

"You don't have to explain anything. The important thing is

that we have a new plan that will serve not only us, but all of humanity. The world deserves the chance we'll be providing."

Marios was in a much better mood than he'd been in for months. "We will enjoy a good sail together, my friend, and we will set things right for a new beginning."

Reza clapped Marios on the shoulder as they approached the roundabout and the turnoff that led to the harbor where *"Scarlet"* was berthed.

There, at the end of L-Dock, was a beautiful sailboat. The mast was made of a sturdy aluminum, glistening with a shiny, white polyurethane finish. The brightly shined stainless steel shrouds and stays that anchored the mast to the teak-decked, white hull with navy blue pin stripes were an indication that the yacht was in immaculate condition. Every line and every sheet was coiled in a shipshape and Bristol fashion. The deck hardware was top-notch. The heavy Andersen winches used to trim the yacht's large sails gleamed in the east Mediterranean sunlight.

Both of the Iranian men stepped aboard. Marios unlocked the companionway hatch before going below. Reza followed him. Both men sat at the navigation table. Marios pulled out a chart covering the whole of the East Mediterranean and pointed to a location southwest of Pylos, Greece, in the Ionian Sea.

"Here, this is the spot where we will accomplish our own brand of a mission for humanity," said Marios.

"How long will it take to sail there?" Reza asked.

"This time of year, maybe three days. If we are lucky, we'll have a gentle south wind the entire voyage. In summer, the winds are stronger, but from an unfavorable direction that would result in an upwind beat the entire way. Even though we'd be moving faster through the water, our route wouldn't be direct, thus taking much longer."

Reza nodded, taking in all the facts and details. He'd never been on a sailboat of any kind, but welcomed the chance to participate in something that would be meaningful. Until this moment, he thought that accomplishing something for mankind died the day the facility at Natanz was destroyed. For a time, Reza was lost and without purpose. However, now, after becoming acquainted with Marios and the impossible task he'd been assigned, Reza was eager to assist his new friend in turning the whole situation around.

"When we arrive at our destination, we'll load the dinghy with the jerry cans of extra diesel and some water. The trip to the Island of Olives shouldn't take more than about two hours," he said, pointing the route on the chart from where they would be scuttling Scarlet.

"I cannot assure you that I won't get seasick on the way to our destination," Reza confessed. "I've never been on a small boat. Not in the sea anyway."

"Don't worry, my friend. The weather forecast is for a steady ten knot breeze out of the south. We'll be on a beam reach the whole time. There shouldn't be any swell or high sea, and Scarlet will move very fast on this point of sail. I will show you. Everything will be fine.

When we arrive, there will be no reason to hesitate with our plan. We'll both load the dinghy, and you'll stand by with the motor running while I open the sea cocks that will eventually flood Scarlet. We'll stay nearby to confirm she'll be headed to the bottom before motoring off for a new start on life."

"Seems like such a waste. This lovely boat," said Reza, looking around at the first-rate, hardwood and polished stainless in the main saloon below deck of the classic Swan.

"We have a higher calling, my friend. Shall we?" Marios said, gesturing to the companionway leading topside. "Let's get underway."

When Marios poked his head above the companionway hatch, he was staring into the barrel of a Beretta 9 MM 8000D Cougar, wielded in the hand of Snake. Marios had never met Snake, but anticipated such an encounter, only not at this moment. He raised his hands above his head.

"Who's that with you?" asked Snake.

"My friend, Reza," Marios answered.

Snake shifted his position so that he could see better, then shouted down to Reza, "Keep your hands where I can see them."

Marios started to move.

"Freeze! Now, slowly back yourself down below and keep your hands where I can see them. That's it, nice and easy."

Once all three men were below deck, Snake had the two Iranians sitting across from him in the saloon with the Cougar trained on them. He'd nearly forgotten about his previous objective to intercept Coolhand. Marios told him the entire story of his involvement with Heydar running Reza at Natanz.

"This turned out better than I ever could have imagined," Snake said to both of them. "Two birds in one go. So, you're the Iranian engineer who likes to run. That was one helluva watch Heydar fixed you up with. I never met him. Didn't even know his name until yesterday. Who was faster, you or him?"

Reza was too shaken to answer. He'd been through so much in the past couple of months, he thought he might have become at least a little more hardened, but he'd never had anyone point a gun at him, which he found unnerving.

"I asked you who was the better runner, you or him?" Snake repeated with an angry snarl.

"He was," said Reza, remembering the man he thought was his friend.

"That's better. Now, gentlemen, it seems we have a problem. One easily solved I should think. I can't let either of you go and we can't have a nuclear device loose for the taking. Maybe even worse, we can't allow it to be detonated somewhere, unless of course, that somewhere is a shit hole in some fucking desert where you people come from. Any suggestions?" Snake paused. "Naw, I didn't think so."

CHAPTER 32

12 January 2012 - Limassol Yacht Harbor, Cyprus

Mark watched as Snake lowered himself through the Swan's companionway hatch. He took note of the pistol in Snake's right hand, then thought about the vinyl pouch with the drug he intended to use on Snake. Not much of a match for a tactical situation like the one he was facing. Regardless, he took it out, leaving the duffle he carried on the dock.

The floating dock was fairly stable, with the exception of a tendency to undulate beneath Mark's footsteps, a reminder that he'd need to be careful when boarding the sailboat. Thankfully, the forty-four-foot Swan was a heavy, solid craft. Mark raised himself aboard and onto the fore deck. He wanted to keep an eye on anyone who might emerge from the companionway hatch.

He was going to work his way slowly toward the main cabin top, when he noticed the large fore deck hatch was propped open.

He lowered himself down to the opening in order to hear what was happening below decks.

After what seemed an eternity, Mark decided he'd heard enough. Snake was holding the two men hostage. Mark had to think quickly and come up with a plan that would allow him to accomplish what he'd set out to do when leaving Israel. He needed to keep Snake alive.

Mark didn't know that Marios and Reza were going to scuttle the Swan along with the nuclear device. He did know that the two men being detained by Snake were the key to preventing a tragedy, so he focused his attention on neutralizing Snake.

Mark grabbed a heavy, stainless steel winch handle from its storage location on the Swan's mast, then he worked his way aft, just above the main companionway hatch forward of the opening. He took advantage of the blind spot to conceal his movements from those below. He knew that with his approach, anyone emerging from below deck couldn't see him. They'd have to turn all the way around in order to look up and forward.

Mark reached down to a taut line cinched tight against a cleat on the cabin top. With his eyes, he followed the line forward. It was a topping lift for the staysail boom. *Perfect*, he thought before unwinding the line from the cleat and dropping the end of the boom to the teak deck where it made a startling noise.

"What the fuck was that?" Snake shouted, then pointed the

pistol in Reza's face. "Sounded like it came from up above. Go see." Snake pointed the gun forward, toward the forepeak where the forward hatch had been propped open to let in fresh air.

Reza got up and worked his way forward.

"What do you see?" Snake demanded.

"Nothing yet."

"Push that hatch open and look up there. I want to know what the fuck that noise was."

Reza was shaking with fear. He looked back and saw Snake with the gun trained on Marios. For the first time in his life, he knew what it meant to see blood in someone's eyes. Snake's were the manifestation of such a vision.

Reza propped the hatch all the way open and stuck his head up. Mark anticipated what would happen and looked back over his shoulder at Reza, giving him a shush with a finger in front of his closed lips. Mark was thankful that Reza complied.

"Well, what's going on up there?" Snake kept persisting.

"Seagull," Reza shouted back down at Snake.

"What?"

"A bird. A seagull must have dropped a shell on the deck."

Mark gave Reza a hand gesture to go back below deck.

"It was nothing," Reza told Snake, feigning relief. Just as he said this, Mark yanked on another piece of running rigging that caused one of the large diameter winches mounted on the cockpit combing to spin with a loud, metallic ratcheting sound.

"What the fuck! I'm going to take a look myself. You mother fuckers don't move," said Snake as he worked his way to the companionway stairs.

Reza made his move at the same time, which caught both Snake and Marios off-guard. Startled, Snake spun from midway up the steps holding on with his left hand and shooting with his right. He put a slug in Reza. "I thought I told you mother fuckers that nobody moves," he shouted while still climbing with his head turned, looking down at the frightened Reza.

Mark long abandoned any idea of using the drug weapon Rina Cohen gave him for taking care of Snake when he saw the Cougar pointed at Reza. He focused his thoughts on how best to disarm Snake, deciding the heavy, steel winch handle was his best option.

"Coolhand, you better stay put or runner boy here is going to take a round, maybe even stop breathing, too, but not until his heart pumps a gallon of blood all over this boat first."

Mark hung the winch handle in his back pocket, hoping Snake wouldn't notice.

"Alright, runner boy, show me how to disarm this fucking thing. Now!" shouted Snake.

"He doesn't know anything about it," said Marios.

"Shut the fuck up. Who asked you?" Snake shouted as he shoved himself over to the Swan's navigation station, seeking out the control panel for the device.

"I wouldn't advise tampering with any of that," Marios warned.

"Who the fuck asked you? Shut the fuck up or runner boy gets it." Snake glanced over to Coolhand and said, get your ass over there and sit on the floor by Benedict Arnold, or runner boy is gonna be pumping blood all over the place."

With his hands in the air, Coolhand made his move to comply and true to form, Snake waved the gun around while simultaneously fiddling with the controls at the navigation station. Suddenly, a loud beep emitted, distracting Snake for a split second. He pulled the trigger of the Cougar still trained on Reza while Coolhand made his move. With the winch handle, Coolhand swung at the backside of Snake's head. Snake looked up at the instant of Coolhand's swing and the two men made eye contact before everything went black for Snake.

"It is ARMED!" Marios shouted. "We've got 72 hours before the device detonates."

"Gone," Mark said, looking up at Marios, acknowledging Reza's death.

Marios nodded but hadn't yet figured out who Mark was and what he was doing aboard the Swan. He did realize that the two of them must be on the same side in this peculiar drama, or else Marios would likely be dead.

"What about him?" Marios asked, looking at Snake laying on

the floor and still breathing.

"I've got other plans for him," Mark said. "By the way, I'm Colonel Mark Reynolds, United States Air Force. I go by Coolhand, and this asshole, here, is responsible for the death of one of my dearest friends. His name is Randy Wormwood. Works for the CIA, and you must be Marios."

"Guilty," said Marios, holding both palms out with his arms hanging at his side. "Farrokh Reza Khadem," he said, pointing to Reza's bleeding form on the cabin sole. "We were just becoming friends. His life turned upside down in recent months…"

Before Snake began to stir from unconsciousness, Marios and Mark quickly exchanged what they knew about Natanz and Wormwood's involvement.

"We've got a problem," Marios said with a sense of calm that made no sense. "This boat is now a ticking time bomb with an armed nuclear device set to go off in less than seventy-two hours."

"Can it be disarmed?" asked Mark.

"I don't know. We never discussed that option and I don't have the technical knowledge to try it."

"What options do we have?" Mark asked, trying to remain calm.

"Reza and I were going to scuttle this boat in the Med's deepest trench, but I'm afraid we won't get there in time.

"Is it possible?" Mark asked.

"Yes, possible, but..."

"Let's roll! Nothing else will matter if we don't get moving," Mark reasoned. "I've sailed before and we must do this." Mark shot up through the companionway and punched the starter for the axillary diesel. On his way back down the companionway, he pulled the MV-ULTRA pouch from his pocket and quickly shot Snake up with a maximum dose.

"Help me with this asshole," he said to Marios.

"Gladly."

They left Snake on the dock and decided to come up with something more elegant for their friend, Reza.

Mark and Marios set sail for Pyros immediately. Marios used the onboard GPS unit to fix a position over the previously calculated coordinates for deepest trench in the Mediterranean. The most painful part of the exercise was their deceased companion, Reza. They decided to carefully wrap his body in the storm jib and let Scarlet take him to the bottom with her when they reached their destination.

They paid close attention to the time-to-destination function, and seemed to be ahead of schedule until the evening when the wind tapered off.

Marios was a skilled sailor and Mark was an agile crew mate. At sunset, they launched the yacht's biggest spinnaker and kept her speed up during the periods when the wind backed and the velocity slowed. Scarlet performed wonderfully. On the third day, they weren't sure they'd make it, but an afternoon squall accompanied by some skillful sail trim and a steady helm got them to their destination with time to spare.

From the dinghy, they watched the beautiful yacht as it blew the remaining bubbles from its interior on its final voyage, plunging its way down the 17,280 feet to the bottom of Calypso Deep, off the coast of Pylos.

EPILOGUE

February 2012 - Lachi Bay, Cyprus

The two men sat on a patio enjoying the warmth of the afternoon sun.

"Tom Mooney," said Mark, thinking that by throwing the name out all by itself, he might get a reaction from the man sitting across the table from him.

Marios turned his eyes from the view he was enjoying and looked to see what kind of expression Mark wore after saying Mooney's name. He paused, setting his afternoon cocktail down on the table, then reached up, rubbing both temples before leaning forward and lowering his hands back to the tabletop.

"Tom started asking lots of questions about things he shouldn't have been meddling in. Old history. I tried to help him. I thought he was a good officer. I never met his family, but we used to meet for coffee from time to time," Marios said with a tone of remorse. "What do you know of Tom?"

"He was a friend. We trained together back in the States and worked on a couple of projects together over the years. So, you're telling me you had no involvement in his death?"

"No. I wished I could have somehow stopped it from happening," Marios told him.

"What did you mean about 'old history' then?" Mark asked.

"August nineteenth, nineteen seventy-four. Amidst the turmoil that threw this island into a quagmire of dysfunctional government, the U.S. Ambassador, Roger Davies, was killed by a stray bullet shot directly through the window of his office in the embassy. I was in Beirut in those days, just getting started. I'd heard about what was happening in Cyprus, but didn't pay much attention to it. For some reason, like a bull dog, Tom bit into his own investigation and the circumstances of strange coincidences full of the kind of violence that killed the ambassador."

"I see. He didn't let the sleeping dog lie. So, you think maybe someone was afraid Tom would find something, so they capped him?" asked Mark.

"I don't think about things I can't change. I don't want to speculate what happened to Tom. He wasn't shot, by the way. He was stabbed in the neck. His death was reported as..."

"Yes, I know. Suicide. I didn't buy it. Not him. Thomas K. Mooney was a standup guy," Mark stated.

"How does a man stab himself in the neck?" asked Marios, not expecting an answer. Instead, he picked up the butter knife from the table in front of him and maneuvered it toward his own neck working out the mechanics and angles for generating enough force to penetrate his jugular. Marios set the knife back down and looked back at Mark.

"What will you do now?" Marios asked.

"Disappear," replied Mark. "Snake and his CIA and DIA buddies managed to ruin the life I had going back in the States. I'm invisible to all of them, but might be of use to certain people and certain organizations."

"I can see that as a possibility. I believe we are men with good instincts. The world is becoming more and more complicated each day. It will take people with good instincts to keep the peace."

"I believe you are correct," Mark said, tossing a copy of the Cyprus Mail across the table to his Iranian friend. "C-Section. Page Two."

"Small Earthquake In Aegean Wakes Residents - No Reports of Injury or Damage," Marios read the headline.

"Now, flip to A-Section. Back Page."

"STUXNET Unraveled," was the title of the article. Mark watched Marios's eyes as he read through the first lines of the article. "It says the team at Symantec and Kaspersky Labs spent quite a bit of effort on a forensic analysis of the STUXNET virus and determined the results to be inconclusive as to the source of the Malware and how it infected several computer networks," Marios commented.

There were no reports from any news coming from Iran. Nothing.

"Iran must have decided to go underground with that threat they put out there," commented Mark.

"Well, when the 17th of January came and went, there were a whole bunch of people wishing they hadn't spent their life's savings on airplane tickets out of Tel Aviv," Marios said chuckling.

"What will you be doing now that you seem to have severed ties and your contacts think you're dead?" Mark asked him.

"Disappear," Marios said.

Both men looked across the table at one another and nodded before raising their glasses of Zivania.

"To Disappearing," Mark said.

"To Disappearing," Marios replied.

The End

Glossary of Terms

A-10 - Originally named "Thunderbolt II: by Fairchild Aircraft, but later dubbed Wart-hog by the pilots who flew it. The low altitude sub-sonic aircraft is powered by twin turbofan engines. It is U.S. Air Force's "Close Air Support" attack aircraft, originally designed as a cold war era anti-Tank weapon system

ACMI - Air Combat Maneuvering Instrumentation

ACTD - Advanced Concept Technology Demonstration - speeds high tech developmental capability to the field on short timelines.

AEGIS - Ticonderoga Class Navy Destroyer ship based combat system

AEOI - Atomic Energy Organization of Iran

AFRL - Air Force Research Labs

AOC - Air Operations Center

ATM - Automated Teller Machine

AWACS - Airborne Warning and Control System

Carbo - Carbohydrate

CIA - Central Intelligence Agency

COMACC - Commander of Air Combat Command - Four Star Air Force General

COMMs - Communications

DARPA - Defense Advanced Research Projects Agency

DFAS - Defense Departments Financial Accounting System

DIA - Defense Intelligence Agency

DoD - Department of Defense

DP Iran Co. - Data Processing Iran Corporation

DSN - Defense Secure Network

F-111 - General Dynamics Viet Nam era two seat swing-wing supersonic fighter bomber

FAC - Forward Air Controller

FACE - Fighter Aircraft Communications Enhancement - description found on open source website

Freqs - Radio Frequencies

GBU-28 - Glide Bomb Unit - version 28 - 5000 pound laser guided weapon. Bunker buster bomb used in DESERT STORM

GPS - Global Positioning Satellite

HUMINT - Human Intelligence - information gathered by human operatives

IAI - Israel Aircraft Industries

IRIB - Islamic Republic of Iran Broadcasting

Iridium - Motorola's Commercial Satellite Communications Link

IT - Information Technology

JUCAS - Joint Unmanned Combat Aerial System

KIA - Killed in action

Ku Sat Link - Ku frequency band satellite communications

Lance Corporal - Fourth level rank for junior enlisted Marines. The first level of opportunity to supervise and train other soldiers

LED - Light emitting diode

LEO - Low Earth Orbit

MIA - Missing in Action

MID-VIEW ULTRA (MV-ULTRA) - Top Secret Specialized Compartmented Information Label for a Department of Defense experimental "Mind Control" weapon

MKULTRA - Top Secret DoD program experimented use of LSD as a weapon - tested on US Military personnel

MISIRI - Ministry of Intelligence and National Security for Iran

MIT - Massachusetts Institute of Technology

MO - Method of Operating

MSL - Mean Sea Level (altitude in feet)

Naval Petty Officer - Non-Commissioned Officer Rank for U.S. Navy enlisted personnel

NSA - National Security Agency

OGA - Other Government Agency

Oblique Imagery- High Altitude Imagery usually acquired by Low Earth Orbiting Satellites or U-2. Images acquired from an angle to the side of the subject as opposed to directly overhead

OPSEC - Operational Security

OPSO - Operations Officer, usually second in command to the Squadron Commander

PIC - Peripheral Interface Controller

POLAD - Political Advisor to the Commander

RAND - Research and Development Corporation

RF - Radio Frequency

RFID - Radio Frequency Identification Device

RISC - Reduced Instruction Set Computing

RPM - Revolutions per minute

RQ-170 Drone - Small stealth UCAV

RTB - Return to base

SAF/IA - Secretary of the Air Forces International Airman Program

SAR - Search and Rescue

SGLI - Servicemen's Group Life Insurance

SMT - Surface Mount Technology

SPAWAR - US Navy Space and Naval Warfare Systems Command

STUXNET - Name given to computer malware worm detected on Siemens control systems designed for Iran's uranium enrichment program.

SUV - Sport Utility Vehicle

T-1 - Combines 24 x 64 Kbit/s channels into one single channel

TS/SCI - Top Secret Specialized Compartmented Information

U-2 - Single seat High Altitude Reconnaissance Aircraft flown above 70,000 feet that can carry imagery sensors and a Signals Intelligence Suite (SIGINT) and simultaneously capture and disseminate data in real-time

U-235 - Uranium isotope making up 0.72% of uranium found in nature. It is usually made from the more common U-238

UAS - Unmanned Aerial System

UAV - Unmanned Aerial Vehicle

UCAV - Unmanned Combat Aerial Vehicle

VSTOL - Vertical/Short Takeoff and Landing aircraft capability

WiFi - Wireless Fidelity - Internet connectivity

ZSU-23 - Soviet era rapid fire 30 millimeter anti-aircraft gun

Note from the Author

Thanks for reading *A Dangerous Element*. Please be sure to rate and review this book on your favorite site, so others will know what is in store for them. Also, feel free to friend me on Facebook at LambPDXauthor, or visit my website at GSLambPDXAuthor.Webs.com.

About the Author

Gregory S. Lamb is a retired military officer. The settings for his novels are inspired by the places where he lived and worked while serving in the armed forces of the United States. He is married to his wife, Cindy. The Lambs live in Portland, Oregon and have three grown sons.

Other Books from Gregory S. Lamb

THE PEOPLE IN BETWEEN:
A CYPRUS ODYSSEY
Through the voices of an American-Cypriot family, the tragic and heartfelt modern history of Cyprus comes alive.

A GHOST NAMED MANKY
Josh Carson opens this campfire-style story explaining to readers how his dad, Bruce "Kit" Carson, is a master storyteller. Kit Carson tells his pre-teen sons the tall tale of a ghost named Mason Manky.

2013: A STELLAR COLLECTION
By Oliver F. Chase, Val Vogel, Sorin Suciu, Raymond Vogel, Ryan Attard, Amber Skye Forbes, Gregory S. Lamb, *Ky Grabowski, & Heather Hebert*
This FREE collection is a group of short stories written by AEC authors. It is a tribute to the hard work they've given AEC Stellar Publishing, Inc. in our first year of business.

Other Books from AEC Stellar Publishing, Inc.

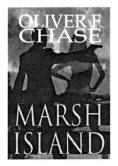

MARSH ISLAND
By Oliver F. Chase
Phil Pfieffer is an ex-Army Ranger turned private investigator who must outrun a psychopathic hit man, henchmen, ferocious sharks and even imprisonment to close the case. *Marsh Island* is Book 1 of *The Hirebomber Crime Series.*

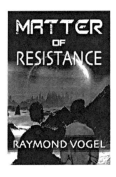

MATTER OF RESISTANCE
By Raymond Vogel
The science fiction imagining of a former rocket scientist, *Matter of Resistance* pushes technology and human nature to the limits as it chronicles our Mars settlement's struggle for independence from Earth. Top scientific, military, and literary minds are all fans of this "instant SciFi classic."

FIRSTBORN
By Ryan Attard
There's a war raging between the forces of Heaven and Hell; and, as if he didn't have enough to deal with from his own issues, his sister has chosen the wrong side. Get hooked into following the misadventures of Eric Ashendale in this first full length novel of *The Legacy Series.*

THE SCRIPTLINGS
By Sorin Suciu
Merkin and Buggeroff are Scriptlings, learning to cope with capitalist magicians, quasi-magical computers, a wandering tribe of monosyllabic demigods, and sometimes-invisible goats. *The Scriptlings* is a laugh-out-loud contemporary fantasy written for geeks and mortals alike.

MINUTES BEFORE SUNSET
By Shannon A. Thompson
This first book in the *Timely Death Series* was released in May of 2013. It tells the story of two young adults whose entanglement may tip the balance between the forces of light and dark. It was recently chosen as a General Fiction Book of the Month at goodreads.com.

WHEN STARS DIE
By Amber Skye Forbes
Shadowy figures haunt Amelia's days in Cathedral Reims, and they are waiting for her to join them. Will the dangerously attractive priest, Oliver Cromwell, be able to protect her and the ones she loves? *When Stars Die* is the first book in *The Stars Trilogy*.

To learn more about these and other great books, visit: www.AECStellar.com

If you enjoyed this book,
please take a few moments to place a review online.
This is the absolute best way to support a writer – either by
sharing your praise with other readers, or by providing your fair
perspective on ways the author can grow and improve their
writing ability.

Thank you!

CPSIA information can be obtained
at www.ICGtesting.com
Printed in the USA
FFOW03n2101090114
3043FF